Dear Corpus Christi

*For Maurell
with love
Eve 1/15/02*

Eve La Salle Caram

1-800-878-3605
e-mail: sbright1@austln.rr.com
www.plainviewpress.com

Copyright Eve La Salle Caram, 1991.
All rights reserved.

Second Printing, 2001

ISBN:0-911051-59-7
Library of Congress Number: 91-066435

Plain View Press
P.O. Box 33311
Austin, TX 78764
512-441-2452

Books by Eve La Salle Caram

Dear Corpus Christi
Rena, A Late Journey
Wintershine
Palm Readings, Stories From Southern California (Editor)

All flesh is grass,
And all its beauty is like the flower of the field.
$\qquad\qquad\qquad\qquad\qquad$ Isaiah 40: 6

With grateful acknowledgement to The Ragdale Foundation and to The Corporation of Yaddo.

With Graditude

Thanks to my mother, Lois,
for her aspirations
and to all of my family, friends, and teachers
who have inspired and encouraged my work.
A special thanks to my daughter,
Bethel Eve, for her loving support
while I was working on this book
and for her blithe spirit.
Thanks to Robert Love Taylor
for his help with the manuscript
at the Ragdale Foundation and after;
and among those close to me, particular thanks to:
Marnell Jameson for her editorial expertise
and for giving so generously of her time and talent.
Thanks also to Frances Grimes, Lola Hovei,
Lori Mass Hultman, Roberta Kanesfsky,
Mary MacFadden and Kate Crane McCarthy.
Thanks, too, to Florence Janovich of Sensible Solutions
for believing in this book
and for her guidance and advice.
And thanks to Jacqueline Piatigorsky,
an early reader, for enthusiasm which spurred me on.
Deep gratitude to Carolyn Waller
for her lifelong friendship
and to all in her big Texas family.
Thanks to Susan Bright, a nurturing editor
and publisher, and to Plain View Press.
I also salute my mentor-guides,
Cecil Dawkins and the late William Goyen.
Dear Corpus Christi is dedicated to all of you.

My thanks to Susan Bright, Sarah Bolz and Louinn Lota for their help in making this tenth anniversary edition of *Dear Corpus Christi* possible. I am very pleased to have it and hope to be in touch with many new readers.

E.L.C.

Part One

" ' Pale horse, pale rider,' " said Miranda, "(We really need a good banjo) 'done taken my lover away.' " Her voice cleared and she said, "But we ought to get on with it. What's the next line?"

"There's a lot more to it than that," said Adam, "about forty verses, the rider done taken away mammy, pappy, brother, sister, the whole family besides the lover."

"But not the singer, not yet," said Miranda. "Death always leave one singer to mourn. 'Death,' she sang, 'oh leave one singer to mourn.' "

Katherine Ann Porter
Pale Horse, Pale Rider

Upstate New York

Is it still spring in March there? Oh very near the beginning with little green leaves popping out on the pin oaks? And in the fields outside of town, the wildflowers, those pale pink ones and butter cups and, up the country, bluebonnets, and then those deep blues, bluets, Aunty used to call them (that's so Texan). Aunty was from Shreveport, but during thirty years with Uncle Leeland, contracting job to contracting job, she picked up a lot of Texas talk.

Where I am now and in late March, too, it's still snowing; I have a bad cold and hurt all over, hurt in my bones. My grandfather used to say, as he lay on his sickbed on the sunporch (he had cancer, his face eaten up with it, I cotton swabbed it every day with the stuff the doctor left). "The future's right here, darlin', a lot of the country's done for and I don't know why you want to go away." Well, of course, I was young and I had to and it was exciting and is, still, but I think it may now be, as the poet said, that the center's shaky or maybe even shifted. Is that my blue-funk-middle-life-late-winter sickness? I think of myself as a hardy type, think other people get sick, have accidents or operations or even serious malaise. Corpus, I'd like to see you. You know that. But now it's not just miles between us.

Or miles between Joe and me. What lies between Joe and me now is all pure spirit—oceans and stratospheres of it, an everlasting country, though hard for the living to reach.

Joe, Corpus, is an old friend whose life—when he was well into and nearly through it—with mine finally magically linked.

Of all the little frame basementless houses in a "just folks," on the fringe of a "poor folks," neighborhood, ours was always the nicest. That was mostly because of Uncle Bo's love of gardening and his flare for decoration. And because my grandmother and my mother, too, were experts with a needle and a bolt of cloth, although my mother, a musician, hated sewing and complained.

Palm was the name of our street, although most of its trees were pin oaks; some houses did have fat stubby palms in their front yards. In ours only slender trunked pecans shot up through the carpet grass and in back the willow Granddaddy planted the year we came surprised us, it grew so tall, and a big chinaberry hung over the porch we used to eat on and over the lattice work fence with gates that Uncle Bo had painted a bright rose shade he called Watermelon. Uncle Bo liked to make up the names of colors and had a predilection for loud ones he thought the neighbors had never seen. "I like to surprise people," he often said, though shock would come closer to what he did.

From month to month we never knew exactly what was going to spring up out of the flower beds. When I was in my middle teens, he planted the one out back with banana trees and black roses, and the roses were nearly black, too. My grandmother, who didn't know what to think, all of us confused her—the world was becoming a puzzle— took pictures of me standing in the middle of them wearing the dress she'd worked on all summer. I went out on my first date after; I was late to have one and maybe she took the picture because she thought it was the only one I was ever going to have.

I can still hear her saying to my mother, "All summer long we had nothing but bananas and black roses, the roses not even looking like real flowers, but like some cheap cloth kind you could buy at Kress's and the bananas too green and hard to eat."

"Well, he doesn't like to be common, Mama."

"But it scares me, sends my head reeling. I don't know why, but I wonder what uncommon thing he'll think of next."

What he thought of, and I'll tell you about in my very next letter, was to try to bring a girl and then a man, both of whom I think he may have loved, into that house. That was real odd to most people who lived in what you were then, Corpus, and he finally couldn't, couldn't bring himself to marry the girl either. And his nerves broke over it. Over it and Grandma's death.

The vine that wound through the lattice work on the front porch was common enough, the bougainvillea. For the longest time I thought Uncle Bo had its name; he had been christened Evansten Fletcher, and since nobody was gong to say any of that, we just called him Bo, though nobody, not Grandma or Aunty or anybody else, knew where Bo came from. You'd have thought Grandma would.

On the New Year's Eve that I turned fifteen, the one before the autumn when Grandma took the picture, I walked around the porch and out into the front and then into the backyard and right into that bed, though no roses were blooming in it. I was wearing the black evening dress Uncle Bo had bought me. I wasn't going anywhere, the dress was another of Bo's extravagances, but I felt as if I was and to a whole lot of places, too! "God," my best friend from high school, who still writes from where she is now, just told me, "when the rest of us were in our Lichenstein's Budget-Floor $29.95 specials, you waltzed around in designer dresses and tried to enter rooms like a model, though you wobbled more than we did in high heels."

From as early as I can remember, Uncle Bo liked to dress me as if it was my destiny to go everywhere, to places far from Nueces County, out of Texas, even; he'd been to California when he was in the navy (was stationed there) though he never got overseas. He'd often tell me, "I'm getting you ready, Baby, for the world."

I can't remember why I was alone in the house that evening, New Year's Eve and the day before my birthday; we had celebrated that noon with a big dinner. We always celebrated my birthday on December 31st, although I was born at 12:01, January 1. My grandmother wasn't yet sick; maybe Uncle Bo had taken her for a ride down on the waterfront around the yacht basin. My grandfather had died just the previous summer. My mother was with my stepfather and away. When I was small Bud had been a safety engineer with a nearby refinery, but then he'd gone off in the army to Alaska, had been in battle in Attu and when he came back, limping, for he'd been shot in the leg, the refinery was shut down. So he became a land salesman for Tennessee Gas which was covering the country with pipeline; that is, he traveled across the country and tried to talk farmers into selling their land. Because of school I couldn't travel with him and my mother, so I stayed in Corpus with my grandmother and Uncle Bo.

The war was five years over when I was fifteen, my family reunited for the first time since I was small, Aunty with us as often as not; after Uncle Leeland died she married again, but it didn't take, Granddaddy's things still in the house and the ghost of him everywhere. Although my mother and Bud traveled, they came back summers and for a few weeks at Christmas and lived in the garage apartment in back of the house. Bo never would rent it. Bo went into insurance and what we thought of as a "good" job, which meant that it was secure and paid enough money and had nothing to do with whether or not he liked it; he didn't "like" it at all.

Bo hadn't minded his work before he went off in the navy; he refused to go into Uncle Leeland and Granddaddy's contracting business, too much he said in the way of mathematics and camping out in winter, though in the middle thirties he and my mother had come to South Texas with them; my mother became the music teacher for refinery children while he ran, more or less happily, though he grumbled, the refinery town's general store. And although the Depression gripped the country, Grandaddy and Uncle Leeland did all right putting up buildings and bridges after they found their way from hard-hit Arkansas to the Texas coast.

No, I don't know where everyone was that late December twilight or what happened later. Earlier Aunty had certainly been around; at four o'clock in the afternoon we'd sat down with soup bowls full of ice cream and cake. Once the house was empty, I suppose I slipped on the evening gown. I don't know; I only remember lifting the big taffeta balloon of a skirt up by a row of beading and waltzing around the yard. I was barefoot, mind you, and carried the shiny spike-heeled sandals that Uncle Bo had also bought me, in my hand, speaking aloud in the stillness to the rose bed, bereft of flowers and to my life which seemed all ahead. "Hello, hello," I called. "Hello college, Europe, New York."

I wasn't the only girl in town who spoke to a future; a lot of the ones I knew whispered hellos to the boys they were with on the bluff that jutted out over the shrimp boats over on Ocean Drive. Years, half a lifetime, lay ahead before I found Joe's love, but I imagined, and even then, envied those sweet whispers and embraces (cheeks against cheeks, hands that traveled across skin and into hair), but my hello, I thought then, was bigger and reached farther. I figured Dallas, about 500 miles to the northwest of us, was about as far as most of the daydreams of the girls I knew ever got. Uncle Bo had outfitted me and I would go farther, though I didn't yet know where.

The very next summer a Tennessee Gas airplane took me across the continent to visit my mother and Bud in New York. I didn't, however, go out in Corpus Christi, at least not with a boy, (which was, then, the only kind of "going out" that mattered) until very nearly a year later. His name was Ben and he was new in town, half Jew somebody told me and not even a Texan. He'd come to Corpus Christi all the way from Kansas; tall and good looking, wavy, dark hair with olive skin and green eyes with thick, almost girlish lashes. As far as I knew, he was the only boy in our high school who'd read both Tolstoy and the Brontes; he represented what for a long time, until I was well into adulthood, I believed lay north of Dallas, a glittering, but mostly peace-loving and literate world.

A word-loving world. In the beginning was "The Word." You taught me that. Remember?

Hey down there, do you still have Buckaneer Days in April? Could I walk the seawall? Take the steps all the way down to watch the pirate ships come in? How I'd like to hang around one of those booths the high school kids used to run, as we waited for Jean LaFitte, selling kites and homemade candy, a lot of divinity as I remember and sour limeades. I made that by the gallon without a drop of syrup. "Keeps the blood down, you know," I'd tell people who came to visit from other towns: Port Lavaca or Palacios. "Here in Corpus helps keep us cool."

"How're you, Travis and John, hey, want to spend some of that pocket money?"

"Well, maybe, what you selling? Kisses?"

Oh, could I come? Wear a strapless dress in the noon sunshine, feel my shoulders burn? April this year brings nasal voices and snow like in

Switzerland, a big wind blowing it up outside the windows where I write, like smoke. Oh, to be in the Texas sunshine, down there near the Bluff, selling coke, lime or lemonade! Just like I used to with my good friend, C.C. (yes, her initials were the same as those in Corpus Christi.)

C.C. and I spent all our free time together, met between periods at school and, afterwards, we'd walk over to get the bus for Chaparral Street, listen to the honky tonk music blasting across the fair grounds, talk our worries out with one another while drinking cokes. On the evenings when we went out, we'd often double date. C.C. went for a long time with a boy named Travis who turned out to be a looker, though he certainly wasn't then and I kept on seeing Ben.

As likely as not we'd been to a Bette Davis picture. One time Ben said, "I hope you won't take this as a compliment, but when you turn your head to the side like that in this neon light, you look a little like Bette Davis; something about you is like her." (He thought complimenting girls, like our Texas boys did, was dumb.) And I said, "I certainly don't take that as a compliment, for while I admire Bette Davis as an actress, I think she is ugly as sin." And he would say, "Oh, I didn't mean it that way, exactly."

And after an awkward silence, C.C. and her date, Travis (more likely than not) would ask if we wanted to go to one of the water front drive-ins. I forget what they were called, but they were all lined up on that street just off the drive by the seawall where our booths were on festive springtime days and had names like Ship Ahoy or Treasure Island or The Bucket. Once we got there, we'd look around first thing and call to people we knew; sometimes we even got out of the car and ran around. But, most likely, just the boys would get out, in our case, just Travis; the rest of us would just sit there and smile and call and wave.

Next day the reports would fly around school. "Last night at The Bucket, Nancy was with Erwin, Patsy with Jimmy, C.C. with Travis (again), Elizabeth with Ben." Once the preliminaries were over and the report for the next day had registered, C.C. and Travis ordered hamburgers. Travis, who was then a pale, pimply-faced tow head, always blushed as he said, "Without the onion," and then turned even redder as he asked, "How about you, C.C.?" And she'd say, "I don't believe I'll have any either." And Ben and I sat very still through all of this—we didn't talk or even smile at each other; each of us sat poker straight and looked right ahead.

Because he'd bought it with what he referred to as his "Tombstone money," Travis called his souped up car The Stone. His father owned a monument business, on the wrong side of town we all thought, though half of us lived there. As we sat in The Stone, pulling on our sour limeades in the September heat and later chewing on the straws, Ben would tell me about Kansas. I didn't want to say anything to him about where I'd lived before we came to Corpus Christi, for I was ashamed of the little refinery town. I thought of it as real low down, probably the ugliest and smelliest hole in the United States. I can still hear my mother saying, "If the world was flat instead of round, it would stop right here."

Except for Bud, nobody in my family actually worked for the refinery and I was glad of that, though it was most certainly refinery money that paid them, Leeland and Grandaddy, the builders, and my mother, the music teacher. I thought of Bo as "the supplier." They all did OK until the war came and shut the refinery down and took the men away, but I never wanted to go back, not even for a day.

I did make conversation out of it, though, sometimes, used it to fend off certain boys.

High school dates always ended up in one place: on the bluff that overlooked the shrimp boats just off Ocean Drive. While C.C. and Travis made out, and for a long time they were crazy about one another, I'd spend my time, as often as not, talking a blue streak. "How do you remember all that?" whoever he was would ask me as I went on pulling myself out of the clinches, as gently as possible so as not to hurt his feelings or make him mad. "You sure are a talker." I'd be telling all about Uncle Leeland, he was the pride of the family, and because he drank so much, also its earliest disgrace and Aunty, who always had such a good time, and finally about my Uncle Bo, who never married, most people who lived in you then thought he was the odd one, who brought some fine things and a little beauty to the refinery town. In addition to lumber and hardware, he started to carry Haviland China and several good lines of furniture, including Duncan Fyfe. "How do you tell all that?" whoever he was would ask me, and I'd answer, "I don't know, in our family we just tell stories, just talk." I started to say, "You can remember a lot if you don't want whoever you're with to paw you."

Ben was different; when he kissed me I liked it a lot and just wanted him to go right on. And I kissed him back. Word got out about that, but we never had more than ten or fifteen minutes. If C.C., whose family was strict Methodist, was home one minute after midnight on Saturdays, her dad, a white collar worker at the Post Office with an unused history degree from Rice University and not some red-necked vigilante, would be on the porch with a gun.

Do sixteen-year-olds go to that bluff anymore? Do shrimpboats still dock there and do they bring in a good catch? We surely had all the shrimp we ever wanted. Bowls just loaded with them at Christmas, the big jumbos stuck through with colored tooth picks for me to push into grapefruit or arrange on plates. As often as not, we'd have a crate of grapefruit somebody had brought up and left with us from the Valley, the Ruby Reds, they called them; they were almost red inside and they were sweet too.

At Christmas we ate ourselves sick on boiled shrimp, and on oysters, fried and on the half-shell and every other way. We always knew somebody with a boat who kept it in the basin and found some excuse to board, and before you knew it, we'd made a party; we'd dance on the decks and play cards in the cabins and there were always cokes or maybe a little bourbon, bourbon sours in December, or boiled shrimp and beer. During the holidays, if there wasn't a yacht basin party, there'd be a Mexican supper somewhere with freshly made tamales. One way or another, you'd get that good food.

At any time of year you could go to North Beach and I liked to, though some of my friends thought it was tacky (all the sailors from the naval base hung out there) where you could buy corn on the cob and ride the Ferris wheel and swing out over the bay. When I was on it, tipping back and forth near the top and could see the town lights for miles in all directions, some of them coming, I realized, from that smelly little town which formed me, I thought about going North and East to Europe maybe, and most certainly, to New York.

And now, here I am with Joe away from me, having accomplished very little of what I intended, and in one of the places I reached for, and a damn cold part.

Do you remember how I used to throw messages—scrawled on Dixie cups that I unfolded and labeled page one and page two—over the side of the Ferris wheel, how on sticky summer nights, the air almost too heavy to breathe, I'd just let them float? "Hey, there it goes!" I'd yell. "Hell, I want to get out of Texas."

Travis would call up from the bottom, "What's the matter, isn't it hot enough for you?"

"Yeah, yeah, it's hot. I want to get out of Hell."

"My name is Elizabeth," my message would say, "and I go to high school here in C.C. I like to go to shows and read long novels and walk the beach and seawall, for miles sometimes, and eat and drink and dance at boating parties. And I like to swim too. Write to me and tell me about where you are and how you like it and what you do."

I'd squeeze all that on a Dixie cup and toss it.
Now I'm trying something much harder, to send messages the other way.
I see my grandfather on the sun porch; his cancer took two years. I

painted his face every day. Every day he'd say, "Honey, why do you want to go running? The future's here. If you stay right here, the world will come to you someday."

God, I'd give anything for a fat grapefruit with some boiled shrimp stuck on it or a half gallon of sour limeade, I'd drink it in the snow. Or ten minutes of Ben's kisses, or just one or two. Or to hear Travis saying, "I don't believe I'll have any onions, how about you, C.C.?" That or anything. He's gone now, the first among us. I don't remember which war took him. He was a handsome senior, after his skin cleared up and tanned and his shoulders filled out and his hair grew. He left us, though. "This is a backwater." That's the last thing I remember him saying. "I'm going to come back and get my girl and get out of it." The girl, by that time, wasn't C.C.; she tried to hide the hurt before she and I went off to college and I'll tell you how, soon.

Have you ever read a more disgustingly homesick letter? Oh, but, I'd give anything for the taste and sound and feel of you, your voices, your kisses, for a North Beach Ferris wheel ride that would go on for a long time, or maybe, never stop, turn me again and again toward those little refinery lights and the Gulf of Mexico where I once wrote messages and dropped them over your sometimes smelly, sometimes sweet and sultry bay.

Hollywood, CA

Well, it's taken me some time to get back to you and I've crossed a lot of miles and many thousand, over decades and decades, in memory.

First of all, in catching up from last time, never mind that neither of them had mothers. The thing was, Travis saw more clearly than she did the difference between a Downtown Methodist and an Assembly of God member—his tiny church was on a gravel road just off the highway to Alice and on the far inland fringe of town—or between the offspring of a man with a degree from Rice University and a tombstone cutter's child.

"It won't work ever," he said to her the day she talked about going to The University of Texas. "I'm never going to go there or to any place like it." C.C. was going to major in art so that she could teach it, nothing she liked better to do than draw.

"You could come to see me," she told him. "And at night you could go to college here in Corpus. It would be OK to go to—" And she named it, the junior college none of us wanted. To stay in you, go to school in you, Corpus, was to go to sleep, like a little death, like being left behind. "You think The Stone would make it?"

That just came out; his getting mad was the last thing in the world she wanted.

C.C., I believe now, was really in love with Travis. Love, I've found out, has no regard for ages, but I couldn't have thought that then. Couldn't admit her ready. Or that Christmas she mounted our loud pink steps, "¡Caramba!" or "Hot Damn," Bo called the color, she had come to say goodbye.

I was packing my bags for college. In just a few months, I would be back I told her. We would write all the time and be close; never mind that the college was in New York.

But she had moved away from me even then, had been funny all summer, buying slinky dresses instead of shirtwaists and bangle bracelets which she had never before worn, and peroxiding streaks in her hair.

Began going out with boys who were older, out of high school, grown men some of them, even with an officer or two from the naval air station. I never could find out exactly where she met them, though she threw out an allusion or two. The son of someone T.J. had known at Rice; (T.J. was her father). Now a handsome twenty-four-year-old naval lieutenant and a visitor in the real estate office where she'd taken a summer job.

Two years later, on that same porch when we were both home for Christmas and strange to each other, she showed her tiny diamond to my mother. She hardly looked at me. It was a year after Travis had taken another girl and gone away. "Why, C.C.," my mother asked, "you getting married?"

"Yes ma'am."

"Why, have you thought about it?"

"Yes ma'am."

Corpus, if I came back to you now, would I know you? Or in unfamiliar buildings and on superhighways, just be lost in tangle? As you can see from the letterhead, I left that cold place I was in and, as they used to say in the movies, came on out to "the coast."

Los Angeles is still pretty—if you don't think about what it is, even the brown haze that hangs on the horizon during certain sunset hours—a city of flowers and balding mountain tops and Spanish voices and many flat, dark faces (I imagine a gentle acceptance in some of them), large sections that are, at least in the daytime, like sleepy little towns. When I ride a Sunset Blvd. bus past pink and blue buildings, one of them devoted entirely to some latter day religion, I think: Why I've come full circle, this is Corpus Christi, but my, how it's grown, even the palms are taller, and how much more it has now, though it all looks worn and more than a little shabby, but so much time has passed, I guess we all do.

I know, of course, that only something about it is like, something sent from here, maybe, that got stuck in the culture.

Your palms were thick, Corpus, and except for that bluff half a mile or so back from your seawall, you had no hills of any kind. Yet, ever since I arrived here, stepping first off a Greyhound bus and then onto a city bus, I've been overwhelmed by the familiar. Again and again I've said to myself, I've always known this and yet I never even saw it in the movies. Paris, Rome and I grew up on shots of New York. But Hollywood Blvd.? Never. Since I was always geared to radio, did I miss those pictures? Why does it seem I might have been young here?

We had no mountains in South Texas and only a little of the same vegetation, oleanders, with their milky poison and the bitter leaf castorbean, yes.

Corpus, you were certainly duller, flatter, bleaker. Yet, here, too, I find scary, barren places. On one side an inhospitable desert, on the other a cold and treacherous sea.

I never thought of the Gulf as treacherous. As often as not, it seemed sluggish, though, of course, on stifling late summer and early fall days hurricanes grew out of it.

The Driscol Hotel, where the seniors had their dances and I hear that's gone now, sat up on a bluff, wind whipping around it, blowing hard enough to tear hair out of the head. I always tied mine up in a scarf. Tyrone Power, who was a big movie star, stayed there; he was in the navy and several of us from the refinery town rode the bus over and went to the movies, then hung around in the Driscol corridors just hoping to get a glimpse and when we never did, grew bold enough to write love notes and stick them under the door.

My note, though, only started as a love note. I managed always to put love off.

Dear Mr. Power,

I think you're wonderful and a good actor. I'd like to meet you someday. Or talk to you on the phone. And might if I came to Hollywood.

Do you know of any jobs there for a young person with an interest in radio drama? Working in pictures would be all right, too, though I'm mostly interested in sound.

Four or five miles south of the Driscol, the Church of the Good Shepherd, Episcopal, though the Spanish architecture made it look Catholic, or "The Shepherd of the Roses," as my friend, Bartola, a wild Mexican boy I'll tell you about later, called it, sat on a shelf of its own. The young blonde minister's name was Reverend Rose (no one said "Father," which possibly gave Bartola his title) a man with pink cheeks and straw colored hair. I only remember Reverend Rose in white, though, surely, in the course of our liturgical year, he must have worn other colors.

I went every Sunday to the Young People's Fellowship and to Evensong, the service I loved best and after spending twenty-five years as an atheist-agnostic, still do, though today I don't know where I'd find one or who I'd take along. Back then, C.C. as often as not, went with me though her membership was with the Methodists downtown. We played board games and down in the rec room, danced to songs like "Harbor Lights" or "Twilight Time," tunes that seemed to go on in you, Corpus, after the rest of the country forgot about them.

But we came for the simple service, too, which without a choir, we sang, kneeling on the crimson velveteen cushions and looking out at the tall, clear windows at the palm branches swaying in a dark wind. The prayers were to God and all bright angels to help us get through the evening in a world shutting down. What I liked, the idea I liked, though I never spoke of it, was that the few of us there, young and ignorant as I knew even then we were, could help God and the angels with that.

Keep watch . . . with those who work, or watch or weep this night, and give thine angels charge . . . bless the dying, sooth the suffering, pity the afflicted, shield the joyous; and all for thy love's sake.

I can't remember now what the old prayer was but it had this same idea. Shield the joyous.

We prayed for ourselves to be shielded then.

Couldn't help what we felt and people can't, can't help their feelings, the life rising in us.

Caused me to sing every morning on my way to the bus stop and after school to run as fast as my strong legs would carry me, sometimes still singing, between the rows of pin oaks to our house.

Bud always said my voice should be trained.

In the house my grandmother lay on her bed doubled up with pain in her stomach no doctor could abolish, no amount of morphine deadened. Weak as she was, she managed to get by us when we weren't looking, pull the step ladder out of the closet in the kitchen, climb up it and reach for the top of the cabinet where Bo thought he had the "medicine" out of reach. In the late afternoons he would stand over her bed asking if she'd like this or that for supper; for a while everything we ate, from macaroni and cheese to oyster stew, was made with milk, and he and Aunt Rena would fix it, Aunty laughing. She was always full of laughter no matter what was going on. "I never saw any proof that life is serious," she'd tell me.

Were she and I, then, among those to be shielded? I asked that question back then.

Today if I went to an Evensong I wouldn't have to ask. But where could I find one? And who could I take along?

I long ago lost track of Bartola Perra and wonder if he's still living. Somehow I never thought of him living long. I don't know why. He wasn't frail looking, only thin with pockmarks. He wasn't accident prone.

Not long ago I heard a terror story about him, heard that last year on the corner of Hollywood and Highland, with a throng in front of Mann's Chinese Theatre watching, watching TV stars arrive for a premier, (not watching Bartola), he was shot through the heart.

Probably just a story although they say he handled cocaine.

"Spic-Wop boy," people said back in you, Corpus Christi, meaning Mexican-Italian (or "Eye-talian") and he was mostly Mexican I think. He wore shirts in bright colors, silky looking synthetics, tied up high like I used to tie mine, all of his mid-section and some of his stomach showing.

"He wants to do you-know-what with his own sex," my friend, Lana, had told me, but in those days I didn't, had only the sketchiest idea of what "you-know-what" was. I knew the sailors who went to North Beach on their Liberties were from lots of places, California as well as New Orleans or Pensacola and that Bartola struck up friendships with some of them, "went off," as he put it, with this one and that, and that sometimes they bought him things.

"I know this town," he'd tell me, "and I show it to them, Baby." Then he would wink and tell me how he showed them the bluffs on the far side of the seawall, his favorite, a deep cavern directly beneath the church, "The Shepherd of the Roses," as he continued to call it, that he was sure no one knew but him.

I wondered if he had an eye for our young minister. And sometimes when we sang or prayed or chanted "Shield the joyous," I wondered if Bartola sat down under the bluff and if he heard and who it was we protected, Reverend Rose or him.

"The person who bought this for me," he'd tell me as he ran his fingers over a silky lapel, "the person has good taste."

Some days he put on lipstick and rouge and a big gold earring, not a fad then, like a movie-star pirate or a movie-star gypsy or a boy-girl. A joy-boy. Into joy, yes, wanting to find it and at the same time, scared he might, scared he couldn't stand it or, worse, that he'd have to steal it and then not be able to stand it and then get caught.

Scared and hiding away a lot of the time, but also receptive. And we were all a little like that; I was like that, but most of the kids I knew wouldn't admit it, so that those who sat around Bartola in speech class got up fast when the bell rang, got out of the room in a hurry.

"He's a disgrace," my friend, Lana, whispered one day just before she disappeared. Lana lived in the house just behind us. Remembering my family chronicle, which I'd learned mostly through my mother and from Aunty, I didn't worry about disgrace; I figured I'd been born in it.

"Elizabeth," Bartola said as I dropped my books slowly into my book bag, we had speech together for two semesters, "Elizabeth, I need to talk to you." We had both had to give speeches in which we used our hands and both gave one on trimming hats. I put flowers on a big white leghorn, he outlandish satin bows on a purple velveteen beret. "I don't care that they all go; you're the only one I care about. They are all so, so—"

"Dull," I said. "And they're afraid of their shadows." Then I grinned at him for he looked surprised.

"You think that, too?" He lifted one of his eyebrows, so black I thought he might have dyed it, and I nodded. "Did you know I went to North Beach last night? Want to know what I did there?"

Here the kids who stand, hands on hips, on Santa Monica Blvd., are often shirtless and seem to like it that way, smiling much of the time, looking happy as if nothing pleased them better than to hustle. Calling out to everybody. Old, young, male, female.

"Hey, lady, I like your body!"

The other day I asked C.C. when I wrote my yearly letter on funny paper I bought as a joke, Sodom and Gomorrah written across the top like a letterhead, if she remembered Bartola and if back in those church days, she thought he'd heard our chanting. She'll probably think I'm nuts.

Asked her, too, if she thought we helped shut those days down.

Now, as then, the world closes.

Here in this improbable place, limos, coliseums, baths, I think of Rome—a poor small town by comparison—of apocalypse. In the summer, fire falls from the air and in the spring whole streets have purple trees. The church I sometimes visit has no children and only a few young people. Cecil B. DeMille, once a member, gave it the Ten Commandments he used in the movie and they're still in the narthex though somebody ripped off the plaque that went alongside.

"I hope they sold it for food instead of coke," the Korean Father says. His church feeds the hungry, opens its doors to the displaced, the jobless and homeless, the addicted.

When I lived in you, Corpus, my church going ran alongside my Grandmother's dying. She was a lifelong Methodist, the other people in the family not members of any church though all believed in what they called a Higher Power and most, like Bo and my mother, in taking communion once in awhile, "joining with The Body," as Uncle Leeland said, though most of the time, whiskey was all he took into his. When I was a child he would leave me at the Episcopal church for Sunday School two doors from the place where he drank, could bring his own bottle, and sometimes where he met women, and all this time, you understand, he was married to Aunt Rena and loved her. He was like all of us, split up that way sometimes, or at least, and how I hated it, like everyone I knew.

I promised I would tell you, but still haven't, have I, about Uncle Bo?

Later

For you to know anything about Uncle Bo, you also have to know about his attachment to my grandmother and how he cared for her through her terrible sickness which began shortly after the start of still another war. The Korean, this time.

I was a senior in high school; during the summer I had, for the first time, flown across the country, to join Mother and Bud, and got my first look at New York. In October, the same month that Grandma began to complain of pains in her stomach, I began regular attendance at The Good Shepherd and Marion Van De Meyer, my Communications teacher, gave me nearly full responsibility for running the radio station at school.

That time preceded so many changes: graduation, our move from Palm Drive and good-byes to many. Some of my friends moved away for jobs or to get an early start on college and half of the boys I knew enlisted in the army or navy.

At the end of my senior year we moved into a new house in a better neighborhood; we didn't own the house, merely rented, closer to The Good Shepherd which had been a bus trip across town. The church building itself, an unadorned white stucco, gave me a sense of protection, of peaceful harbor.

Bo put our old house on the market because he said he couldn't stand to hear Grandma still in it, he claimed to hear her for months after she died, and in July he sold it, so that two years later, when C.C. came back to show her ring off on our newly colored steps, (¡Caramba!), it was a different house, all the old ghosts gone, she came back to.

"I had to get us out," Bo told me, "your grandmother gone and not gone, clinging on to all of us, trying to take me with her." I, too, thought I'd heard noises, felt threatened. And I blamed her, blamed her for not dying the way I thought she ought to. She went one sticky June afternoon, screaming and clawing the air, saying she wasn't going to do it. Threw up and then choked on part of her insides.

The diagnosis for what she'd called "nervous stomach" came in December; she'd had some stomach trouble for as long as any of us could remember, always eating Tums or asking for soda or Pepto Bismal, but it had grown much worse that fall. She suffered all through those last months in a blue speckled house dress she'd sewn up herself and in an amber one just like it except for the color. "I can just 'wrench' these out myself," she said.

She "wrenched" them both out every weekend and lived her death days in them, alternating the colors all winter when the sun was, as she so often said, pale in the "windas," stopped in June just after my graduation from Corpus Christi High School to which I wore a yellow sashed white eyelet dress, the sun so bright then, all of us, except her, consumed by heat.

My mother always says it's our destiny, and she means by this our family's destiny, to die in summer and that it's fitting then, graduation time.

But I've always thought my death will come, that I will fall into it, a few weeks or months after my New Year's birthday, just before the green budding of trees and before the delicate colors of wildflowers that just crop up in the grass, pale pinks and deep blues and buttercups, that my body and brain will know better somehow than to try to make it through another year and with both earthly and celestial help I can quit before even the earliest breaking of the Texas spring.

Maybe that's because I read somewhere that people who die of natural causes do go a few weeks or months past their birthdays. My old friend, Joe Copeland, did it that way, died a little past his New Year's birthday, in his last years we had celebrated together; Joe had just raised a window on a whole lot of brightness and something, a question, a wonder, had sprung up between us, suddenly as wildflowers and as fragile, gone as quickly, surprising him and me.

That winter my grandmother asked me to paint her face every morning. "Paint my face!" she'd cry and I'd think: Oh, you are so vain and difficult.

"Paint my face!" When she'd yell that my mind would drift to thoughts of Ben, to being held by him or to dancing down in the Shepherd's rec room, to the way the music made me feel there, like I could fly.

Paint my face. My grandfather had asked for the same thing, but he'd meant medicine and she meant make-up, a special cream I filled wrinkles in with, then make-up base, plum colored lipstick, powder, plum colored rouge. "Come here," she called, "Come here and help me."

I translated that to mean: Pay for the room I give you. My mother sends a check every month, I wanted to call back, my mother pays you.

My grandmother came from people for whom life had been hard and who were stingy with one another, not with food or money so much, though they were careful with those, as with affectionate words for one another and with touch.

Only now I remember that frail saving sweetness I sensed rising in her—I try now to focus on what was saving in us—that I saw play around her lips when she sewed.

My grandmother cared for me through work, the only way she knew how, sewing for long hours, making when I was small, among other things, beautiful organdy dresses. I remember a peach one for Easter, knotted with purply ribbons and garlands of flowers. Though dressmaking was her gift, she cooked for long times, too, making angel food cakes for all our birthdays and homemade ice cream, stirring the custard for that on the wood stove we had when I was little, collapsing in a chair when she was done, calling out to Grandaddy and Leeland to pour it in the freezer and crank it, otherwise uncommunicative, looking martyred, the way she thought she was supposed to be.

One Sunday afternoon when I refused to go on a drive with her, she said I wasn't grateful. The drive was as much a ritual as church and she put on the same hat and gloves for it. And each week Bo, in jacket and tie, got out the DeSoto and drove her down by the waterfront, then up the bluff past all the expensive houses on Ocean Drive.

Aunt Rena, seldom around much on weekends, was off gadding somewhere. She never met a stranger, struck up friendships on city buses and in public parks and movie matinees and during the course of a week, visited more people than the rest of us did in a year. Black hair slicked back and gold-looped earrings stuck through her ears.

On Sundays when she was gone, Bo and Grandma both took pleasure in talking about her and I can tell you, in sometimes calling her some awful names. It was in Grandma's side of the family to do that, the English-German side, not the Black Scot.

I wrote or did homework on Sundays and on that particular one was well into what I thought might be a hot radio drama, a ghost story, I always did turn out a lot of them, copied from the format of "Inner Sanctum," a show that always began with the sound of a squeaking door.

"If it weren't for me and for your Uncle Bo, do you have any idea where you would be?" My grandmother asked the question in a level voice and pointed toward the street with the cane she had carried since the summer she broke her hip, before I had even begun grade school.

I threw everything on my desk at her: pens, books and even my ink bottle, all but the typewriter, God knows I didn't want to damage that, and all missed, but the ink and glass made a mess on Bo's newly polished floor.

During the following week I was down on my knees with a steel wool pad, feeling wretched, doing penance. I had just made my first earned radio money from a Saturday broadcast and in addition to trying to get the stain out of the floor, I spent almost all of it on an Elizabeth Arden cream and worked half of Monday afternoon smoothing out the wrinkles in Grandma's face.

"Where's your Uncle Bo?" she asked and I just told her he would be late by a little.

He had called home to say he and Robin Lee were down on the waterfront eating shrimp in a basket. "You tell Rena to go on with whatever she can find for supper; there are pork chops in the refrigerator and you can help her peel and mash some potatoes, Mother can eat mashed potatoes, and open some canned green beans."

"I suppose you would rather be off somewhere with that girlfriend of yours," Grandma said. "She's boy-crazy."

"She's not boy-crazy, Grandma." No, just Travis-crazy, I thought.

I remembered a time when she and I had hung around the lot with the tombstones in it for half a Sunday morning waiting for Travis to finish helping his father carve birth and death dates into several newly commissioned stones.

Travis's father, a big, silent and I thought probably sullen man, finally pulled five one-dollar bills out of his apron pocket and handed them to Travis who grinned at us and within minutes we were in The Stone on our way to North Beach, Travis's arm around C.C., her head on his shoulder, both of them in my idea of Heaven.

"Well," Grandma said, "God knows where you go or what you do." She picked up the jar of cream I had bought and put it on the night stand and I took it from her—for a moment I thought she might throw it at me—and opened it, dipped my middle finger in and carefully patted her face. "I suppose your Uncle Bo is running around with that boy from the navy."

"No, Grandma, he said he had to work. I guess he's still at the office." I lied because I know she'd be furious if she thought he was with Robin Lee. She tolerated Jay.

Just about that time the nurse we hired to be with Grandma, I must have known her name but I forget it, poked her head in and said she wanted to talk to me. Did I realize Grandma had insisted she change all her bedding and spoon feed the vegetable soup Rena made for lunch? "I'm a practical nurse, not a maid or a keeper," she told me, and then said I could do the chores she had mentioned or Aunt Rena could. "I realize she's in terrible pain, but I sometimes wish you people would find someone else to help her bear it. The old lady sure knows how to dish out abuse."

I said that if she talked to Bo, he might be willing to pay her a little more, but was immediately sorry I had said it. I knew Bo had just enough for our bills.

"Maybe he'll have to," she told me. "Your grandmother expects too much."

Grandaddy hadn't seemed to have expected anything. "Ellen," he asked, the only time I remember his asking for anything except his medicine, "could you please make a dish sometime without noodles and tomatoes in it? Do you always have to stretch everything?"

She stretched food so she'd have money to buy expensive fabric and patterns, though she often sewed from her own.

Now I remember all the dresses she made and sold, some of them for good prices, and how she smiled when she sewed. I saw that same shy delighted smile the day she discovered that I was on the radio, heard my voice coming out of it and onto the sunporch, with my Saturday broadcast for teens.

"Why, how is it?" she asked, tickled, "that I can hear you on the radio when you are also right here with me in this room?"

"It's a recording, Grandma."

I don't know that she ever understood that.

I considered her a domestic, narrow minded and of little curiosity, bigoted, judgmental and opposed somehow to loving, all I swore I would not be. I only half thought of her sickness as serious and only toward the end as "dying," annoyed as I was when I couldn't play my records or type scripts for my broadcasts and worried that I wouldn't be able to give a successful senior party. Successful ones were loud.

And almost every senior gave one, a brunch after which people stayed to play "Oklahoma" or "South Pacific" on the hi-fi and to air frustrations and dreams, or a coke party, which then meant Coca-Cola, or even a formal tea.

The coke parties, held usually on Saturday mornings, were the easiest and the cheapest and allowed for the most people and I was going to have mine with C.C. We planned to have more than one hundred seniors and to use my house since it had the bigger yard. My grandmother's room, however, was practically in it, so I didn't see how we could have any fun.

"You'll just have to ask for quiet," Bo said, "and tell those who know her to drop in and pay their respects."

I don't know why that came so hard. For reasons that aren't clear to me even now I was ashamed, ashamed almost to have a grandmother, ashamed to be living with her and ashamed most all of her terrible sickness. It ran in families we all knew.

The sickness and our knowledge of it was so awful that I sometimes think we held back or misplaced our true feelings and did cruel, and in the manner in which Bo had formed us, even shocking things.

Did we think of her dying as too common, maybe? He doesn't want us to be common, Mama. And had we all in such close quarters been too much for each other, my mother and Bud back by spring? Bo said so.

Coronado, CA

Grandma died three days after my senior party.

Yes, C.C. and I pulled that off.

Draped all the porches, front and side and even the back patio, with purple and gold crepe paper, Buckaneer colors; our cheerleaders wore purple bell-sleeved blouses, gold satin boleros and sashes. "Colors for thieves," I said to C.C. I always did feel I was one and grew up in the right place, snatching my fun. To guide the guests around the side of the house so they wouldn't ring the doorbell or walk straight through, we made a walkway out of sticks wrapped in crepe paper.

Grandma seemed almost well that day—sat up in bed in a peach colored bed jacket Bo had brought home for her the afternoon he came in late after supper with Robin Lee—smiled, spoke nicely to all who came in to see her and told several she hoped they would stay.

"Elizabeth is a smart girl," she told C.C., "but not always company. Just types."

Here I am still typing and looking out on another bay, shut away from its beauty, although through the window I see the gold glittering on the water, holed up to meet a deadline, forever cranking out radio dramas, this one about adolescence, though it seems more urgent to write to you about my own.

At our party C.C. and one or two others, Lana and Gerry I remember, stayed all day and then that night stayed over. C.C. had several calls from Travis and at midnight, he came to the house and I heard them on the front porch. This was because Gerry had told C.C. that if she wanted to talk to Travis, she'd have to ask him over because she had her own plans for the phone.

We all peeked and saw them nuzzling one another and we heard them, too. Travis, I believe, spoke as little as his father, but his soft voice was very much more appealing and the few words he did use and his very presence, a shy one, said a lot.

"I don't know what to do about you," we heard him whisper that night. Then "I'm in misery." And, of the two of them, I think he may have been the one most in it. And the one who stayed. Both of them somehow were, in spite of their kissing and clinging, a sad sight, not one to watch for long, so after the briefest glimpse, I turned away.

Turned toward the hall telephone and my two other friends, Lana and Gerry—Lana, a strawberry blonde with freckles—she wore a Veronica Lake peek-a-boo hairstyle hoping it would hide some of them and Gerry, a dark, maverick of a girl like me.

Gerry liked to call teachers, always had crushes on the male ones and calling them and pretending to be a poll taker, asked their views on local issues while making thumping noises with the hand she held against the small breast closest to her heart.

That night she also called our famous Baptist preacher, well known on radio all the way to Del Rio, "Brother Blow off," we said, and asked his opinion on certain picture shows—we knew his daughter had to come home from scout camp because she'd seen one—then asked if he thought the Dragon Grill, the newest restaurant in town, ought to be issued a liquor license so it could serve mixed drinks.

Bo, who seemed to feel as festive as we did, stayed in the kitchen mixing his own, even serving us one now and then, a good thing C.C.'s dad never knew it. C.C.'s mother, before she left, drank a lot of Jax beer so drinking, in general, upset him. "I'll never be a drunk like my brother," Uncle Bo said, downing his daiquiri, getting ready to cook short orders.

"Why don't you call up Bartola?" Gerry asked, giggling. "Ask him if he's going to the prom. Ask what he'll be wearing." She saw him, she said, in a sequined dress.

"That's mean, Gerry," I said. "You know I won't do that." I told Uncle Bo I thought we'd all like some scrambled eggs. Scrambled eggs, Bo said, were common. So he baked eggs for us, with hot peppers and cheese on top.

We stayed up all night, of course. Bo, too. Toward morning Grandma started screaming and from then until the end, the agony we were witness to was, for all of us, nearly impossible to bear. The woman we hired to nurse her wouldn't, walked out right after she walked in, early in that day. Later Bo argued with the doctor about giving Grandma heroin.

"Who in the hell cares if it makes her an addict?" Bo asked.

Weeks after she died Bo said he could still hear her screaming; in his sleep he said, that's when he heard her. And when he didn't sleep he heard worse. Heard her dragging what surely sounded like her dead body through one-hundred-degree heat in the Palm Drive house.

I don't know if I heard her or only imagined that I did worn out as I was from my first job which seemed to have nothing to do with anything I cared about, in the fur department of Lichenstein's, typing numbers day after day.

I had hoped to work for KRIS but Dan Rodriguez who had been my assistant at the high school station took its only summer spot.

The man Bo brought to the house didn't look much older than Dan, light skinned, light eyed, a year or two past twenty. The first time I saw him standing in the screen door that separated the side porch from the breakfast room, he was eating a big chunk of angel food cake, Aunty made that after Grandma died, and he looked like an angel, or the way I had always imagined one, sunlight striking him through the branches and lacy leaves of the chinaberry tree.

A mistake, I thought at first, for him to have left California where he might have gotten into pictures. I probably got my ideas of what angels should look like from the movies. But he suffered when he first spoke and held his mouth in a pursing way that changed my mind. "We w-w-w-were b-b-b-oth sa-sa-sa-sailors i-n-n-n San Diego." He got the name of the city out whole. He told me how he met Bo who had run the general store at the naval base and was never sent overseas. Another man, someone else he met in San Diego, brought him to Corpus and to work in Las Hadas, Bartola said that meant "The Good Fairy"—my friends giggled about that—where we had eaten once a month since I was small. Just an accident he said that both his navy friends came from the same place.

I could tell Jay's presence made Bo happy. I had never seen Bo look at anyone like that except sometimes at Grandma and now and then at me. I don't know that it was sexual, in the way people usually think about that, although, I guess, in the truest sense it was, only that there was all this feeling in it.

Bo's love for his family we all knew and he knew, too, was excessive, was more akin to passion, because, or so Rena said, he was the baby and pampered, or because family was something he felt he could never get out of, that it was sinful to even want to.

Now some of this same love spilled over to the boy who looked so much like Bo that he might have been his brother.

Bo never looked at Robin Lee that way, or I never saw him do it; most of the time he looked past her, looked away, as if he was afraid. Yet there was no question in my mind that he considered making her his wife.

He would have married her, he said, as soon as he got out of the service, but since he looked after Grandma and Grandaddy, being the only one of their children able to do it, Leeland and Lloyd both dead and my mother as the only girl considered financially incapable, he didn't know how he could also take on Robin Lee.

Aunty said he could have found a way if he had really wanted to, but I could see his side. Robin Lee didn't make much at Bo's insurance office where she worked as a sometimes typist and filing clerk. She would have been an extra burden and was frail besides, susceptible to colds, a touch of T.B. once someone said, and suffered from continual bronchial trouble. Yet, one humid afternoon, I heard him asking her to consider life with him and with us all.

"Mother would like to have you and I would, too," he told her. Then he said that, of course, her mother would also be welcome. "If you were both just here it would help us all so much." A false smile, the one he wore when, inside at least, he trembled, played around his lips.

They were still sitting at the breakfast room table where they had eaten lunch. I was just outside on the porch, (almost all our rooms had porches), but they didn't know.

When Robin Lee asked where she would stay, he said she could have the little extra room just off the hall near Grandma, between Grandma's room and the place on the porch where Bo slept. Or, if she liked, he said she could stay out with her mother in the garage apartment, Leona and Bud would be gone all fall, though I could tell both by what he said and the halting way in which he spoke that he wanted her in the house.

The bed in the garage apartment, he said, was a narrow double and only really any good for man and wife. Then he said he thought he could get her and her mother a tenant for their house for the time it was vacant, maybe an officer from the naval air station so that when the new year came they would be a few dollars ahead.

Robin Lee's mother had spoken of wanting a change, was known by all of us to like excitement; this might be just as good as a trip. As he spoke he looked out the window, his trembling voice almost a whisper and then stopped with, "Oh, please, Robin Lee."

"I don't see how I could," she told him. Her voice also trembled and her freckled hands, both clutching the china cup into which he poured the coffee. He still hovered over her and I now remember where Aunt Rena thought he got his name. From the "Bo" in "bow and arrow."

Grandaddy or somebody had said he was as bent as a bow, that the taller he grew the more he bent over, and thin as a bow string. Now I watched the string that was him quiver as if arrows would soon be shot off.

My mother, who gave him piano lessons at night and behind drawn curtains so that the neighbors wouldn't know a boy of our family was studying music, said that music and not arrows would come from him.

"If you could it would," he said, then stopped so that I, still eavesdropping on the breakfast room porch, wanted to finish for him. Wanted him to say, "It would make me happy."

"It would," he said, "help Mother. Be a help to Mother and to me."

She dropped the cup then and it made a big noise as it hit the glass table top, but didn't break, though the coffee spilled over the glass and on to the floor. He brushed her shoulder with one of his large knotted hands, and she shook like a little yard rabbit shakes and she was shy and plain as one, a funny girl for Bo who, when he was away from the office, and toward the end, in it, wore so many red shirts and red caps and liked so

29

many things bold. "I'll clean it up," he said.

For a second I thought she might dart out of the room and pass me on the porch, but she stayed put, shaking, the coffee a pool on the speckled linoleum floor. I opened the door then, thinking maybe they needed me to help clear away the tension and as I came in I thought I heard her say, "We'll see."

Finally it wasn't Robin Lee but her mother who refused us. Her mother, or so I heard Aunt Rena say, didn't like the proposed location of Robin Lee's room.

By the time the refusal came, half of you, Corpus, seemed to know that Bo Bell had tried to bring a girl he worked with into his house to live with him there and had even had the audacity to also ask her mother.

When many months later Bo invited Jay to live with us, he pointed to the ribbons of light in the bedroom, Grandma's room that he offered. With Grandma's dresser gone— he had given the dresser to me—he said there would be plenty of room for an easel. Drawing was what Jay most liked to do.

I knew the neighbors would talk about Jay living with us even more than they would talk about Robin Lee. Ever since he first came to our house, Lana's mother asked me lots of questions about him, Lana lived right behind us with her mother and brother, her father, a railroad engineer, dead for years, killed in an accident on the SP. And once I heard Brad, Lana's overgrown and I thought overbearing brother, call Jay a queer. Where had Jay come from, Lana's mother wanted to know and where had Bo met him? Who were Jay's people and why on earth was he living in Las Hadas? Even Lana's mother, who as far as I knew never ate Mexican food, but only collard and mustard greens and the plainest of meat and potatoes, and who had given her children movie magazine names, even Lana's mother had heard about Las Hadas and "that."

Although you weren't a little town, Corpus, not in numbers, not even in those days, you behaved like one.

Bo said it was natural for Jay to live in Las Hadas since he worked there.

"Yes," Aunt Rena said, "but in what capacity?"

She didn't care, was laughing when she asked this.

Still I felt Jay, Uncle Bo, myself, all threatened.

'Oh," I said, "he works as a waiter, handyman, painter." I was quick to give the list.

Still at Coronado

In Las Hadas where we had come for our monthly dinner, we sat at a lacquered table shaped like a tropical flower. Jay had not only done the art work in it and on the red, green and blue chairs we sat in, but he had also painted the mural before us which featured a hillside dotted with pink and blue houses, banana leaves in the foreground, an ocean in the background and a little strip of blue sky. And over it all, a small woman who held a large stick. I had looked at it through several evenings and over a good many enchiladas before I realized the stick was a wand and the woman a fairy godmother. A little magic, a fantasy, Jay said.

I liked the mural and told him so, the way he had done her with just a few curved strokes.

Drawing, not painting, he said to us, stumbling hardly at all over the words, was what interested him most, that and wearing apparel, odd, I thought. Designing clothes was what he really wanted to do; he said he had, in fact, already designed some, had a portfolio he might sometime take to New York.

"I'm going to sell them," he told me, each word as clear as crystal. And I thought maybe he looked into one and saw his future there.

I had never before met anyone with so focused an artistic ambition. In high school I had come in second in the "Most Likely to Succeed" contest. Dan came in first, which was strange to me since he was my assistant at the station, but I suspected he won votes for his position in the Student Council which only made officers of boys, and even more for the wheeling and dealing the kids knew he could do with cars; he even finagled a few spots on our station for them. From my second semester at CCHS I collected all the material and did all the scheduling for CCHS Broadcasting and was sure that radio, either in writing or production, would somehow be my life. My wanting to work at something particular and not just earn a check, was odd to most people and sometimes even to me. I couldn't have explained it and still can't, but ever since I was little and heard voices coming out of our old floor model radio, my grandfather and uncles huddled around it, and only the men listened with consistency, I had wanted to.

When the war was on and the men gone and even Uncle Bo off in the navy, I listened alone. "Portia Faces Life" to "Lux Radio Theater," "Gang Busters," "The Green Hornet" to "Quiz Kids" to "The Life of Riley" and "Fibber McGee and Molly" to President Roosevelt.

Worked to death, my mother spent her days and half her evenings, too, teaching music in the piano rooms provided for her in the public school.

On Texas stations I heard Joe Copeland's show; he had wonderful dramas, even then got his actors from the Alley Theatre in Houston. From earliest childhood, I had been an admirer of Joe's productions. Some of them were musical, his wife, Kate, was a singer, and some were concerned with the news and local issues, but more were dramatic. Except for the news shows, I listened to them all.

Then I met him. The year I won the teen's contest for radio drama and rode the bus to Dallas with my fans and a few winners in other divisions to get my prize.

"Leona Bell's daughter? Why, Elizabeth, all this is just in your blood." And he opened his arms wide as if to embrace me and my mother at that station. Joe was always one for the expansive gesture. "I still remember your mother opening KTHS."

KTHS stood for Come Home to Hot Springs. And no, I don't know why the initial for "Come" was a "K" instead of a "C." My mother's piano music followed by Governor Terrell's voice from the Arlington Hotel ballroom were the first sounds heard over the Arkansas airways at a time when there weren't more than fifty stations in the United States.

"You heard my mother?" I asked him.

"Everybody did. Queen of the Ivories, that's what they called her up there and even in some Texas counties. She played so many places, I heard her years later on an Okie station, WKY, I think it was and that was an oldie."

"Well," I told him, "I know she did once play in Oklahoma. I know she was with KCRC in Enid in 1926."

"Oh, those were exciting times, Elizabeth," Joe said, "an opening up for sound through the west." He laughed that wonderful deep laugh of his that seemed to come from somewhere near the very bottom of him. "She played in those stations outfitted with only a piano and a Victrola in somebody's parlor. Just a tangle of wires and homemade parts, your mother was a part of all that."

I told Joe I had heard that technicians in those early days found it hard to deal with a piano, that receiving sets wouldn't pick up the high notes, that violins were a better instrument for them to work with. "Your mother knew how to handle a piano for radio," Joe said. "Even with that primitive equipment she got almost all the music across."

It thrilled me that Joe Copeland knew my mother. No one in Corpus Christi knew her; once when I was a child, she had played for KOMA in Oklahoma City and KSD in Dallas, but she had never performed on radio in Corpus, or anywhere else in years.

When I came back from Dallas that spring the school almost elected me "Most Likely to Succeed" and the next fall Miss Van De Meyer, whom we simply called "Miss V," put me in charge of our school station. Miss Van De Meyer had been a Wave in the war and her name shortened, the "V" standing less for Van De Meyer than for "Victory."

I didn't know if Jay's classmates had almost elected him "Most Likely To" anything, but I thought he and I had a lot in common, that, like me, he had probably come in second quite a lot. From the outset it seemed to me that the big difference between us was that he had a chance to realize his dreams, whereas, mine, so often and especially after graduation from high school, seemed thwarted.

I was right about that because an oil man who came to Las Hadas admired Jay's mural —Jay was reworking part of it, this rich man watching—and wanted to know what else he had done. "Do you have any pictures?" he asked. Jay was too practical, and he had been too poor, to have spent time painting pictures not knowing if anybody except his friends would ever see or buy them.

He and I are alike that way. Why I have never written anything but scripts.

"No, I don't paint," Jay told the oil man. Never mind that he stood there with a paintbrush and a tin of blue paint in his hands. "I'm interested mostly in drawing and in wearing apparel."

When the man came back a few days later to see Jay's portfolio, he put money on it and said he would arrange for a Dallas show.

Jay beamed as he appeared in front of us holding pottery plates steaming with rice, beans, enchiladas, the tacos and guacamole already on the table. And he didn't stutter once. "Next month," he told us, "I'm taking my line to Dallas."

Bo looked just miserable about that. But congratulated Jay and ordered Carta Blancas for himself and Aunt Rena and a coke for me.

"Bo Bell," Jay said, "I wish you could come with me."

"Well, I can't." Bo could seldom get away from his company.

"Well, then, hang on; when I get back I'll rent that r-r-room y-y-you sh-sh-owed me."

But he didn't as things turned out.

Bo lost his nerve about that. Later in the summer, after some talk started in you, Corpus, he retracted his offer, and right after, bee-lined it to Robin Lee's. And after talking to her, put the Palm Drive house on the market.

I don't know if he did that because he was too often reminded of Grandma's suffering in it or was just too afraid of Jay's moving in. Or was desperate for money to pay off bills.

Or some combination of all three.

I'm going to save the story about it for a little while. And I'm also going to put off the story of his engagement to Robin Lee.

Coronado,
*Flecks of gold
still glittering in
the water and the sand*

My memory moves back and forth among these seasons, but what I have to tell you now is that very late in that summer after we moved into the big house that we rented in those hot, final weeks before I went to college, Bo seemed really dispirited, somehow brokenhearted, always walking around with a drink. I longed then to take off for the East, but postponed making a decision about going since I didn't think Bo should spend the money for my tuition and since I knew I could if I chose, even at the last minute, go to UT.

One unbearably hot hundred-degree sticky afternoon, Bo studied the sketches Jay left and drank vodka, new for him; he had always talked against vodka, but on this day seemed to like it well enough mixed with grapefruit juice, freshly squeezed and poured over ice. A day came, of course, when he liked it any way, and as often as not, just turned up the bottle.

After he finished the drink and put Jay's sketches in a drawer, he went shopping. For years he had, at the beginning of every season, brought home a bunch of boxes for Grandma and for me, and some of the things for me were always for school and some were for dances and parties.

"But what if I'm not invited to any?" I would ask, pulling on the ashy black hair I hated, cowlicked in all the wrong places, even at seventeen I had grey patches, and he would say, "You're going to be ready to go."

Bo, like my grandmother and like Jay, loved dresses and he brought home several beauties, among them a long-sleeved, calf-length black cocktail dress, a cowl-necked crepe, the kind I dreamed about wearing in some cool foreign fall thousands of miles away from you, C.C. He also brought an expensive grey tweed suit and a number of cashmere sweaters that in my mind epitomized what successful young women wore on the job in New York. Then at the bottom of the box I found a pale grey-blue sleeveless swirly skirted chiffon that seemed more like Texas and home

I had all month pored over the fashion magazines which in August, as we sweltered, were always filled with pictures of furs and heavy woolens, the kind of clothes people in South Texas sometimes bought for a season that never came. How well I remember every fall on the first sixty-degree morning putting on a corduroy skirt and bolero, or a jumper, over dark cotton, knowing it would be eighty by afternoon. Playing at autumn, feeling disappointed and guilty that it was not as advertised and as if that were somehow my fault.

I hoped when I left Texas I would be less defective, one of the reasons I wanted to go.

Being what the press said I should be was, of course, easier than trying to discover anything about myself or my region on my own. Cost me a lot of time and as I grabbed onto other people's lives and loves, or wanted to, made me even more thieving than I already was, while deepening shame.

"You can have any or all of them," Bo said about the dresses, "but you have to do something about your hair."

I thought maybe I would have my hair dyed cold black. Once and for all, get the ash out of it. Afterwards I would put it all up on rollers and then, to get the cowlicks out, brush like hell.

I told Uncle Bo I wanted only the cocktail dress, the crepe. But when I held the slate blue chiffon next to me, and I wanted to feel contempt for it, I thought for a moment I might go to college in both Texas and New York.

Was New York the center of the world? I didn't know, only knew that it, the center, was cold.

"Well," Bo said, "you might as well know it. They're all yours. I just put them on my charge."

During those August days he not only drank all the time, he spent money all the time, money he didn't have, granted that most of it was on other people, and a lot on me.

"Decide," he said, "which one you want to wear this evening. I'm taking you and Robin Lee, and" (he sighed) "her mother to the Dragon Grill for dinner."

This time I am now telling you about was late August or early September. Mother and Bud left right after we sold the house in mid-July. Jay was in Dallas and, from what we heard, thriving. He sent us copies of his press releases and a few pictures of his show, but he didn't write. I knew he had been rebuffed, and more, deeply hurt and disappointed when Bo turned him away. He had no idea that we were going to move or where, though of course Bo did finally tell him and sent the address.

But he certainly didn't know on that day when we set out for The Dragon. Or on the sweltering afternoon, some weeks before, when Bo had agreed to marry Robin Lee.

Just as, before that, Bo had no idea she was going to propose.

When we were all seated silently around a long table at The Dragon, we were, supposedly, in the dragon's mouth, sitting right at the tip of its tongue, I was nervous and kept fingering the grey-blue lace of my dress and the matching seashell earrings that at the last minute Bo pulled out of his hip pocket. Here we are, I thought, in the dragon's mouth, right on the tip of the dragon's tongue. And yet where are our own?

Then Bo and I began talking. I told him for the first time and to the silence of the others, that in a few weeks I thought if everything was OK I would go on up to Austin and UT. Robin Lee's mother then interjected (Robin Lee had not said a word since we left the house) "Bo, I want to ask you something. I know you and Robin have set a date for next summer, but I want to know why you have put it off 'til then?"

Bo who had just taken an oyster with a lot of hot sauce on it into his mouth went into a coughing fit and when he came out of it, said he had to wait because he had just put his mother in the ground and was not yet in condition to give himself to a marriage partner, nor was his house ready. He said he always had to keep rooms for my mother and for me and that he hadn't had time to get the rest of the house set up for a bride or to assess anything.

He was, I thought, amazingly articulate for one caught off guard and just before Robin Lee's mother ordered the cornish hen she murmured, "Oh well, I see."

Robin Lee went on calmly spooning her lemon soup in the lamp light, her freckled hand shining; she probably thought she was through with the subject for good.

To break the silence I said I thought the lemon soup exotic (before I came into The Dragon I never heard of lemon soup) that I thought it must be what citrus growers intended beautiful people to eat in Borneo and Madagascar and the South Seas. Why I said things like that I still don't know.

No one responded. Not even Bo. Silence claimed us through the cornish game hen and that great fifties desert, Baked Alaska.

"Well, did you hear them?" Bo asked when we got home. "These brazen women. My God."

Essie Burnhardt's mother was also brazen, and Bo's most regular caller, that is before Robin Lee proposed and he accepted.

The spring before and, in fact, all the time I was in high school, several of the women in Bo's office, of whom Essie was one, called almost every day. Bo grumbled a lot, but liked the attention. Essie, a tall, long-necked, long-torsoed, long-legged woman was rumored, maybe because of all that length, to be very fast on her feet.

Bo took Essie out a lot during that last Palm Drive spring; she had fiery green eyes and, yes, cold black hair, not ashy like mine, not a touch of grey in it, and one weekend took her as far as Monterrey, Mexico. As I remember, they left on a Thursday and when they came back on Tuesday Bo was sulky and Essie looked like she had been through a bad sickness or a war.

Nevertheless, she insisted on showing us pictures of the trip including several shots of her and Bo on burros. A Mexican boy in one of the pictures seemed to be holding Essie onto the animal's back and I knew immediately she had too much tequila in her, I had seen Essie drink tequila. Had probably been drinking it straight. According to Bo, who decided finally to comment, they had ridden the burros to a spectacular waterfall high in the mountains; Essie didn't seem to remember much about the expedition or, if she did, she didn't say.

That afternoon Bo didn't get out the cocktail shaker which was certainly unlike him, and he seemed considerably relieved when Essie decided to go home.

I knew if Bo had cared deeply for Essie he wouldn't have gone away with her so easily. He would be able to do it now if he was young and living his life all over. But not, not the way he was raised, back then.

Well, anyway, on that afternoon back in the spring Essie hadn't been gone for more than ten minutes when he called Robin Lee. I can still hear them laughing in the backyard.

After planting a whole bed of zinnias, each of them working different rows, they sat down at the table Grandaddy built under the willow to stake tomato plants and consumed with great pleasure Rena's perfectly plain—Rena hadn't ever put sugar in it—pitcher of iced tea.

Still typing,
this time in Ensenada, Mexico

In spring Robin Lee liked working in the yard as much as Bo did, but she had an interest in planting and tending vegetables, even carpet grass, while he only cared for his tropical flowers. Hibiscus. Gardenias.

But, clearly, they had a good time together, were even foolish together and about each other in it, giggling over silly jokes and sayings and, sometimes, playing games like peek-a-boo and hide-and-seek, unbelievable even to me as I watched over my scripts from the sunporch, and at their most sophisticated, guessing games about what sort of animals or birds the people at their insurance office would be if they were animals or birds.

Before I became so busy at the radio station Bo played like this with me.

Essie would be a giraffe, Bo said, except that as far as he knew, giraffes didn't drink booze. Sometimes they sang songs in bad Spanish. Bo often talked to an imaginary character he called "Old Spanish."

His conversations with "Old Spanish" are among my earliest memories. Being here on the Baja brings them all back.

"Well, how are you today, Old Spanish... Loco?... Loco in the cabeza?... Oh, you don't say?"

I thought that someday I would put Old Spanish, or maybe Old Spanish and Bo, on a radio show.

"La cucaracha," Robin Lee sang softly into the flower bed. Although she was a shy girl, she was also fey, possessed I was sure by a fairy spirit which was not delicate but strong.

But during the last months of Grandma's sickness Robin Lee stayed away.

Not that she wanted to. She loved what Bo loved and truly. Too much wild creature in her to "love" out of duty. But her mother had never liked Grandma and liked Grandma even less after Grandma got cancer and it took a good hold. Still Robin Lee phoned the house often enough in the evenings.

"I'm going to my room now," I told Bo after I heard them starting. "I'll leave you and your callers alone."

"What do you do in your room all the time?" he asked me.

"Write love letters," I wanted to tell him. And sometimes I did write them, letters to the soul mate I had not yet met who understood me completely and who I believed was surely somewhere waiting. And one or two to Ben.

Uncle Bo, I write love letters, I wanted to tell him. And I touch myself.

In bed before napping I did touch myself, too. Touched that private part of my body I had not read about in any book and which I had not been told about, what it was for and why touching it was so exciting, and for which I had no name. I wondered if I would get a sickness from it and if the sickness would be as bad as Grandma's.

"Well, answer me," Bo said. "What do you do?"

"Work on radio dramas," I told him.

"More spooky stories?"

"Not anymore. Now I'm writing about you." And I had, in fact, started something on him.

"Oh, Elizabeth, be serious."

"Aunty says life isn't."

"Is that supposed to mean something?" Bo stared at me, incredulous. "Life is real, Baby, life is earnest."

I knew if he didn't most of the time think so he wouldn't stick so close to all of us, wouldn't still be selling insurance, making up all those policies and plans.

Later

from a beach house near Ensenada.
I move up and down this coast.

During that final high school spring the telephone was once in awhile for me. I still went out with Ben sometimes, but I hesitated to say yes now when he asked me, knew I would be in for some trouble. It was getting harder and harder to pull away from his kisses. Also my hours at the radio station were getting worse. I couldn't go anywhere or see anyone, hardly ever got to see C.C., it was so late when the place shut down. Most nights I stayed there with Dan Rodriguez; Dan and I had started together in Miss V's radio workshop when we were in tenth grade.

Everybody pointed to Dan as Corpus Christi High School's outstanding Latin American student which was possibly because Dan aspired to be all things Anglo. His father, the town's leading used car dealer, had just bought a colonial house near Ocean Drive. Every week or so Dan drove a different car to school, often a year-old Buick or Caddy. When we finished at the station he'd take me home but sometimes before he did, we'd go down to the waterfront for a coke. One Friday when I was griping about the grind at the station, I suggested we close down early and take a waterfront spin in whatever Dan happened to be driving, an Olds as things turned out.

As we were turning into the drive-in which I now think of as The Bucket, whether or not that was its name, the editor of the school paper nearly ran head-on into Dan's Olds and Dan said a few words that surprised me. Two days later we were an item in The Pirate, the school paper.

Both our names appeared in the column called "Stolen Treasures." Worse, because this column had won a prize in a statewide high school journalism competition, the entry was reprinted by The Corpus Christi Caller Times.

Guess what we ran into? Old Dan Rod in his latest, The King of Rods in a new one. Was it a Mercury? And with a late lady? Was she a McElroy? Was it necessary to sit so close, Dan?

When Ben read that in the Caller Times—he never read the school paper—he called up and said he had to have an answer as to whether or not I would go steady.

"It wasn't a Mercury, Ben," I told him. "It was an Olds."

"Never mind any of that," he told me. Then he said if I couldn't go steady, he didn't want to go out at all.

I said I liked seeing him, but I couldn't go steady because of the demands of the radio station and because of my family. "You know," I told him, "I'm at the station four nights a week and, anyway, my family says I can't go steady."

I lied about that.

"Ever?" he asked, sarcastically. "Not when you're twenty-eight? Thirty-two?"

"Not," I stammered, "until I'm nineteen. Or on my own." Whichever comes first.

"By that time you'll be out of high school."

"Well," I said, "I certainly do hope so."

I was wretched, panicked. Although I guess I secretly thought Bo would be jealous, as far as I knew, my family didn't care.

And no one, with the possible exception of Miss V, gave a damn whether I put in time at the station or not.

"I love being with Ben," I told my mother when she was home Christmas. I watched her green eyes, my tiny reflection in them, watched her brushing her wild, wavy dark hair. "I don't know why," I went on, "why I can't say 'yes' when he talks about going steady."

She couldn't answer.

My mother and I were close sometimes. When she was home we would talk for hours, sitting on the patio or in the garage apartment lying side-by-side across the double bed.

Still, I could never go into detail about the strong feelings I had for Ben. Could only repeat, "I don't understand why I can't go steady."

After which, she was mute.

She just looked at me out of her heart-shaped freckled face with those uncommon green eyes. I thought they were beautiful, that she was beautiful with her green eyes and dark auburn hair.

An old friend just wrote me that he remembered my mother as tall, dark-haired and very pretty, "a dynamic woman of the coastal bend."

"Oh, I just don't know," I murmured.

"Well, you have got years for all that."

All she ever said.

C.C. wanted nothing so much as to go steady with Travis. But he didn't ask her. Then she said she knew it was because they lived on different sides of town. "Still," she told me, "I don't understand. I could understand if I lived on Ocean Drive like Dan does."

C.C. and her father lived on Texas Street in a new neighborhood which was undistinguished and treeless; C.C.'s father bought the house with an FHA loan just as dozens of his neighbors had, on the "right" side of you, Corpus, the "right" side of the way in which you were growing.

"I like it out where Travis lives better," C.C. always said.

"But it's what your neighborhood represents," I told her, "white collar jobs, aspiration, respect for education."

"Oh," she moaned, "the status quo."

The space between them was a gulf as wide as the one between us and Florida. I saw the expanse of it, but C.C. didn't, only thought she had to be with him.

She got literally sick to her stomach, nearly threw up in his yard, when she found Travis with another girl who was, like him, a tow-head and who lived on his own gravel road, just the other side of the frame church they all went to, who came by some evenings to put on a pot of pinto beans, which all day had been soaking, for his and his dad's supper and who sometimes boiled some greens and made a skillet of cornbread for them, too.

Travis's mother had been dead for years, died during an epidemic of typhoid fever, and C.C.'s mother was long gone, remarried several times over with a bunch of children C.C. had never seen, but who were, nevertheless, her half-sisters and-brothers.

The girl's dad drove a truck for a nearby lumber yard and her mother did ironing for people, that and mending and little sewing jobs, running up rick-rack over a dress's worn places, taking up or letting down hems. She couldn't make a whole dress, couldn't sew from a pattern.

Considering the way C.C. had been brought up, it was bad enough that she found Travis with a girl at all, much less like she did with this particular one, him on top of her, her blouse up around her neck, his hands on her tiny breasts.

"I only went in the bedroom," C.C. told me, "because I heard those noises. Didn't know what they were. I thought he was sick in it."

She had driven out to Travis's house on the spur of the moment in T.J.'s old car, of course got T.J.'s permission to do it. She never did things like that, hadn't even had her driver's license long, always held out for Travis's invitations, waited for him to call.

That evening, she said, a spell must have been cast on her because after she parked and went up to the door, she just went on in the house. No one had answered her knock and the door was open.

She had just received some pamphlets through the mail from the junior college and she wanted to show him. The courses in draftmanship she was sure he would want to take. Someone told me that after Travis went into the service he became a draftsman.

I had no drama like that, wouldn't let myself. And what I wrote was always for other people to play.

I wanted, I told myself, to preserve something.

But not to bury it. Not to keep it in the ground forever. I wanted blooms.

But did nothing to nurture them.

I went, hell-bent, on my precious business.

Grandma's work ethic had rubbed off, maybe, or worse: I had inherited some of her witholding qualities.

Still in Mexico
near Ensenada

Bo and I held ourselves back and although she had been through two marriages, so did my mother.

Did Bo drink, I wondered, so that he might let go?

Back in April, before he began to get into drinking so heavily, Bo told me he had an unhappy dream. Robin Lee, he said, had been in it, all done up in white like some bride. What was weird about it he said was that Robin Lee in her fine white dress swung back and forth, like Nyoka, the Saturday serials queen, in an old jungle movie, from the bottom branch of the willow tree. "Only we all know," he said, "that she's no Nyoka. The poor little brown mouse of a thing."

Then he turned away from me to address Old Spanish. "Don't you think so, too, Old Spanish?" When I was a child I half-believed in Old Spanish—in fact, sometimes, still do—kept looking for him, and I told myself I would know him when I saw him, still do, kept looking for him around corners or through windows to the far side of the yard.

No matter that he complained, no matter what his consolation, both the dream and the telling of it pleased Bo, made him feel more a part of you, Corpus.

Bo knew some of what people said. Once he overheard Lana's mother say to C.C., "Find out all you can about Bo Bell while you're visiting. Any man who would paint his house Spic Pink is peculiar."

As he pulled weeds from the flower beds—he was down on his hands and knees—Bo heard. He worked for hours, for whole days sometimes, back there; fastidious as he was, he loved to dig in dirt, do any kind of yard work, but especially work in flower beds and scratched around the zinnias and black roses with his hands.

Later that same week, as he came in the dining room at the Nixon cafe for the Rotary Club's monthly luncheon, and I guess, staggering a little—his company required his attendance, but he hated the gatherings and finally had to get drunk to go—he heard the blue-suited men near the head of the big table whispering about him.

Heard ugly things said, he told me. Though he never made clear just what.

Told me all this as he poured rum in the limeade he had stirred up for the afternoon's guests. All spring he kept asking his lady friends, with their mothers, to the house for Sunday suppers. But I had noticed that for sometime he focused more on fooling with rum and limes than he did with the food.

"They say I'm odd," he told me. "Well, maybe, I am. If that means I'm not like them, the old bastards, I do hope so."

Then in summer, just after they had met at Las Hadas, after Grandma had died, but before Bo decided to sell the house, he related the dream he had about Jay. In the dream he and Jay were both dead and had gone to Heaven. Only Heaven was really California, a beach near San Diego where they sat naked, staring at each other and making pictures, each of the other, in the sand.

"I looked at Jay and Jay looked at me," he told me, "and when we did, it was as if we saw ourselves through a mirror, we weren't in the glass, you understand, but through it, on the other side. "Do you think that's a strange dream?" he asked. "They say I'm strange, you know."

I told him I thought dreams were strange, and yes, this one. And I did think so.

But even at sixteen I saw how innocently he told it.

In the summer Bo invited Jay over some evenings for ice cream. They sat side by side out on the enclosed sunporch which on the walls that weren't screened had floor to ceiling bookshelves filled with books on gardening and decorating, the relief of those subjects broken with fiction, a few best sellers from The Book of The Month Club.

Bo sat in a hard ladder-back chair, he would never sit in a soft chair, Jay in Grandaddy's old oak rocker, a good looking pair, Jay just a little taller than Bo, but both so long and thin, dark-skinned and light-headed, Jay's hair as blonde as sunlight, Bo's nearly as white as Grandaddy's; it had, a long time ago, as everyone said, turned "prematurely."

After they finished the bowls of vanilla ice cream covered with caramel syrup and with pecans picked from our own tree, they took long walks through the neighborhood streets, since there was nowhere else to go.

From the vacant lot on the corner we could all see, when we walked there, Sinton refinery and oil rigging lights. The putrid smell of gas often in the air.

On his radio show Joe Copeland used to talk about viewing lights like that from a distance, from the window of a house, or, more commonly, from the highway in a car, about the mystery connected to them and the ghostly yearnings they conjured up.

And once Joe said to me, once after he had spent a long time in Europe, right after he had come back and come to pick me up in Dallas where I was working and then drove me out into the country, into the fields, "There. There they are," he said. "I love those little lights."

Even then, Joe, I wondered why. And I thought that only a person who was going to leave this country forever could love them.

Oh, but, Corpus, do I mix you and Joe up sometimes? I was, wasn't I, talking only to you?

Well, we could reach them by car, not that any of us wanted to. From where we were the smell of gas was bad enough.

When Bo and Jay came back into the house from their walks, swinging along side-by-side like two school kids, Bo would get out the cocktail shaker. As far as I knew we were the only family on our side of town who had one.

What was it for? A release from timidity? To help us see a little shine on the land? A promise, like the one the preachers gave, that not too many believed anymore, of the end of travail, an entrance into Glory?

"For awhile," Bo said to me years later, after he was finally off the bottle, "the world seemed very flat and dull." He had put the cocktail shaker away. The poison he had poured into it had eventually sapped his energy and sense. Poison it was, but we had all told the stories of our lives over it.

Later

And I can see it so plainly.

The cocktail shaker.

A glass one with one red stripe down the middle and a screw-on top of sterling silver. The focal point of these evenings.

Bo bought it at cost from his own gift shop, the one he had put in the refinery town's general store. During those years, war years most of them, we used it only at Christmas. No one we knew drank anything but beer, though some of the men also took now and then to hard liquor, bourbon usually, which more often than not, they just drank straight.

We came up in the world when we moved to you, Corpus Christi. Though in you, potent drinks of some sort were the highlight of our weekend evenings, just as they had been in the smelly little town.

Around Jay, Bo would refer to our refinery days sometimes. And then, remembering, would tell him stories of the weekends when he and my mother and their friends got together and went honky-tonking in the little clapboard cafes along the side of the highway, those with maybe one neon light and inside a lighted juke box which for a quarter would play five popular country songs.

Oh, Bo wanted to tell Jay all about this. Jay stirred everything up in him, even then I could see that, stirred his memory, excited his imagination. He wanted to tell him things.

Just as in the beginning I wanted to tell Joe.

And now, must tell you.

"The water was new to us," my mother said when she was remembering. "All of us just down from Arkansas and the East Texas woods. When we first came we would swim every night, would pile in the car every evening and take off for Rockport, after Leeland and your Grandaddy were through with jobs and I had taught my last lesson and Bo shut up the store." All of them put in ten hour days. "Finally Leeland even bought a boat and we used to take it out to fish."

Some Saturday nights Bo and my mother and Bo's truck drivers and painters, and maybe one or two others, would go to Ransom Island to dance and drink beer. They would also take me more often than not since they had no one to leave me with and in looking back, I'm glad to have been included, to have been let in on their vices.

The time came, my mother said, when Ransom Island was the only place they would honky-tonk. "The shed out there that sold beer was nice," she said, "quiet, peaceful even, right on the water. You could always hear the water lapping. And there were never really loud people or fist fights like in Sinton or Gregory or other places back in those little towns. We would have to take the ferry north of Aransas Pass and the trip across water helped keep us calm as we were going and certainly sobered us all up as we were coming home."

On Ransom Island they sometimes talked and drank beer and danced to the juke box until nearly morning. Some of the men who worked with Leeland and Grandaddy, when Leeland and Grandaddy were with us, brought their wives and girlfriends and Bo almost always brought workers and their families from his store. One of Bo's truck drivers, a man we called Shorty who delivered lumber and his wife, Gert, and their little boy, Elbert, often came. Elbert and I would sing to the records and dance a little, he leading with big, predictable steps across the splintered floor—all this in an open shed on stilts which raised it high over the water—pumping my hand up and down, copying his father's style and we liked to play like we were his mother and father.

Later on in the lumber sheds he taught me to play like we could do what they did in bed, what it looked like to him; he told me he saw it every night after supper and I thought that was so strange and that what he described was strange, his father lying on top of his mother, but I loved the way what he did to me in the lumber stacks felt, mostly he just rubbed his little body against mine, sometimes after pulling my dress up, or, depending on the season, my shorts and his pants down, one of his legs always moving against me and I suppose, accidentally against that place where I finally touched myself. Got so every day I would say, "Oh, let's go out and play in the lumber like we did yesterday!" And sometimes he would say OK and sometimes he would call for his mother and say, "Mama, Elizabeth is a bad girl and wants to do bad things in the lumber stacks today." And I would say, "Well, you taught me about it, Elbert." And he'd say, "Ummm, she's tellin' a story."

And sometimes he would then turn to me and say, "Elizabeth, you tell stories and one night when you are sleeping, The Devil is going to come to your bed and put you in a sack and take you away."

A Sunday school teacher, I found out later, had told Elbert about The Devil and Elbert had only been to Sunday school once, but that one time carried and lasted as both of us waited for The Devil night after night.

What a patchwork time makes of memory! At Ransom Island we never thought of any of this, but only liked to sing.

"You are my sunshine/my only sunshine/you make me hap-pee/when skies are grey."

That was the song we played and sang the most, and sometimes, even when our dancing was through, Elbert would sing it and pretend he was strumming it out on his toy guitar. Back in Ingleside, and that was the name of our town, we would sing it on street corners, Elbert holding the guitar and me holding a paper cup for donations from the IGA store.

Sometimes Elbert's father and my mother and Uncle Bo would go with us down the steps of the dancing shed and out onto a little strip of sand and then knee high, no farther, into the water. After a dance or two Elbert and I would usually beg to go in and then I, never Elbert, would cry, "Oh, please, Mama, please Shorty, let us take our clothes off and go swimmin'," but they would always say no.

"You young'uns just wade a little, " Shorty would say. "You can't trust the water here. All at once it's over your head."

Then my mother would tell the story, for the umpteenth time, of how Leeland once took them all out in the boat they bought for fishing, took them out from Ransom Island where he kept it, and of how they hadn't gone far when the motor died and a wind came up and it took them all night to paddle back to the shed in the storm and how they then had to take the ferry; there was always that ferry that got us across the water and back to shore.

I would become afraid of the water then and of the dark and didn't see what the grown-ups saw in just sitting there for hours playing the juke box and drinking beer and sometimes I would start to cry.

"Why, are you the same young'un who just a minute ago was beggin' to strip down and go in the water?" Shorty would ask me.

"Here, here," my mother would say, for I embarrassed her as I wailed, "Now you straighten up."

And Elbert would say, "Yeah, Lizabeth, nobody likes a cry baby." And Shorty would pick me up and swing me over his head and cry, "Look up at all them stars, girl, ever see stars like that?" and whirl me around in the air. "Hear all that music?" He would go on, swinging me down toward the steps of the shed. "Let's get to it." Then he'd all but fly up the steps with me and when we were on the splintered dance floor whirl me around some more, his wife, Gert, laughing, then pass me to Uncle Bo who would whirl me and throw me up in the air; once Bo caught me so hard when I was coming down that he sprained my arm, by which time I could see my mother and Elbert coming up the steps. All of this excited and confused me and shut me up and scared me some, too; in the middle of it one of them would yell, "Oh, aren't you having fun?" to make me think I was. By the time Bo put me down, my mother had usually had time to take Fritos and deviled ham sandwiches out of the basket they had brought and set on the table. She might also take out some celery and sweet pickles all neatly wrapped in wax paper. "You children are hungry," she would say, putting the food she had wrapped so lovingly before us, her green eyes gleaming in that face that more and more, because of the way she brushed her hair back, looked like a heart.

If Aunt Rena was along, and once or twice I remember her and Uncle Leeland coming with us, she would bring out a deck of cards. "Want to play Fish?" she would ask us. "I'll play Fish with you." But my mother, who hated cards, never thought to bring any.

Well, anyway, we munched on Fritos as the grown-ups went on dancing, talking and laughing. And louder and louder with all of it as they drank more beer. And, finally, Elbert and I would just give up, would stretch out on the benches built into the walls of the shed and fall asleep while looking at the sky and counting and sometimes giving names to the stars.

Usually, nights were on the hot side, but if a wind came up, my mother or Gert would wrap us in old quilts they had brought along, covers that Rena had long ago pieced together back in Arkansas or East Texas. Then sometimes in sleep the water as I heard it lapping scared me; I'd dream then that we were all lost, drifting in Leeland's boat and I'd pull the quilt close around me.

Rena's mother had done most of the oldest quilt like a star, Rena helping just a little when she was a girl back in Louisiana, before Uncle Leeland met her. Even as a girl she had been married once and before she was seventeen had a child who lived a year, then had to go, died in sleep. This same child had on the day she was born, ripped the womb out of Rena, seeing to it that Rena could never have another.

Some years after her baby died and the baby's father had run away, Uncle Leeland spied Aunt Rena picking berries in a blackberry thicket, or so the story goes, where he and his crew were building a bridge across the Texas-Louisiana border. Leeland dropped everything the minute he saw Aunt Rena, married her a week later and according to my mother, who believes Leeland's spirit lives with us still, has kept her, and her black-Creole spirit, with us ever since.

"So sad," my mother always said, "that they couldn't have children." Sometimes, though, I thought it was because they couldn't that Rena and Leeland were so close to one another. Rena did have two nephews in Louisiana, her dead sister's children, but they were grown men when I was just a child and I thought it was funny that she called them "my little boys." I was also jealous of them, or at least a little.

I always hid when I saw their car coming up our hill as it did only once a year, usually in mid-summer. Aunt Rena would usually find me under the feather bed, that is if I wasn't curled up in one of her wedding ring quilts. "Now come on out here and speak to my little boys, Johnny and his brother." Johnny as the oldest was called by his name. "You all are going to have a lot of fun." I can't remember what they looked like, much less any fun; the whole time they visited I stayed close by the radio and Uncle Leeland, who I sometimes thought liked to listen almost as much as I did. But years later Aunt Rena told me that one of the nephews, the one whose name I never knew or anyway can't remember, carried me on his back to the creek and sometimes even farther, all the way to the spring.

Toward the end of these nights on Ransom Island Bo would talk about Leeland, that is, if Leeland wasn't along, railing against him and all that Leeland had, Bo believed, forced on him in the way of work and ambition. Usually I would fall asleep somewhere near the middle of this; I knew it wore Bo out to go over it again and again and that it was in part because he was tired from the story telling that he had to sleep for half the next day. Mornings after Ransom Island my mother and Bo would let me skip Sunday school and they would stay in bed all morning, wouldn't even get up to go to the door.

With Jay, when he once again told about Ransom Island, Bo would also go over his quarrel with Leeland.

"My big brother would give me these long math problems to work out," he told Jay. "Even calculus sometimes. Can you believe that? Calculus. For me? I would have to struggle with these problems for half a day. And after I finished, Leeland made me camp out. I always hated that, sleeping on the wet ground. 'Come on,' Leeland would always say, 'be a man.' From the time I was little I heard that from him, and yes, from my other brother, Lloyd, and from my father, too. Made me hate them, all of them sometimes, and just want to stay in the house with my mother."

"Why," my mother told me on Sunday evenings when Uncle Bo was getting his stock straight so as to begin another work week in his store, (my mother always got stories to come out her way), "why, they never expected your Uncle Bo to be a builder. Leeland and your Grandaddy were going to build the houses and stores and office buildings, Lloyd was going to finance their venturing a little, you know Lloyd was in the wholesale food business, and then the plan called for your Uncle Bo to decorate and help furnish the interiors. Bo never understood that. That was Leeland's dream. All the rest, the camping out, the math problems, all of that was just to make him part of them. A kind of testing."

"Well," I said, "it was testing of the wrong kind." I had never known Lloyd and loved Leeland and my grandfather, but at least at the time she told me all this, my sympathies were with Bo.

Bo said Leeland wanted him to become some sort of mathematical wizard and that because he knew this, Bo who had no mathematical aptitude, had in the course of two semesters signed up for calculus, geometry and advanced trig. Just one of these courses, he said, made him want to quit the university and near the end of his freshman year he did. Bo's quitting broke Leeland's heart everyone said.

Leeland who had to go to work young and never finished his architecture degree had made a present of Bo's tuition money, had been saving it for years.

I never understood why, instead of quitting the university, Bo didn't just drop all his impossible courses; I always thought Bo should have just stood up to Leeland. If he had, I was sure Leeland and everyone else would have let him finish whatever he wanted to do.

On those nights on Ransom Island Bo went over his side of things. And again, years later, when he went over the Ransom Island nights with Jay.

On one Ransom Island night I heard him crying. I was awake because a norther had come up. All this was on one long ago early October morning during a blustery ferry ride in rain. Bo always had to be at least a little bit high before he would talk much about himself and smashed before he would get out all of what I came to think of as "his story."

Around Jay he always wanted to tell it.

I read somewhere that's how you can tell if you love someone, that if you want to tell him or her your story, you probably do.

Hollywood

Bo told Jay about what a drunk Leeland was or at least told when Aunty and my mother weren't around, and about how he, Bo, was never going to be. "I'll never be a drunk like my brother, Leeland, never act or talk like him." And he never did rant and rave, or swear, like Leeland. Oh, he would say "Shit" over and over sometimes, but that was about as bad as his language ever got. As spring came and Grandma's sickness worsened, he became, I noticed, more and more jittery and some evenings drank so many daiquiris he would slur and distort his words. "Shit" would become "Shut" for example. This was back in March.

One Sunday when he entertained one lady friend and her mother, Essie Burnhardt I'm almost sure now it was, he started making and drinking daiquiris early in the afternoon and went on like this, putting off 'til nearly dark making the supper he had invited them for. He had planned to do a batch of tacos, frying and folding each tortilla separately in a big thick skillet on the stove. His tacos were particularly good ones with piles of chopped green onions and green olives on top of shredded lettuce.

When he finally apologized for supper being late, after eight instead of at six-thirty, Old Lady Burnhardt said, and I'm sure now that's who it was, "That's all right, Bo. We know now that when you invite us to your house for dinner, we should eat before we come."

The Sunday after that he had them all there, everybody: Robin Lee, her hair falling loose around her shoulders instead of in double pony tails as it usually was, and Essie, taller and skinnier looking than ever, in four-inch heels and a black and white striped suit, her black hair shingled, and finally Pauline Honish, of whom I've told you nothing about so far, a big raw-boned girl whose father, before he died, had made money in cotton farming, about all you need to know. And all of their mothers with them. And Aunt Rena was there, too.

Because everyone Bo knew was at our house and Aunt Rena never had her friends there, when the telephone rang, I knew it had to be for me.

Ben wanted to know if I would go for a ride with him. Down to The Bucket maybe.

Just as I was about to leave, I was in the bathroom fixing my face, Bo started. I heard him beginning on Robin Lee's mother and on Essie and Essie's mother, Grandma so sick that day that the nurse had on both sides locked the door and when Bo came out from seeing about her he said, "Mother is not up to visiting with anyone today," and poured himself a glass of straight rum.

Then after Essie's mother and Robin Lee and her mother had the sense to go out the back door and take chairs on the patio and in the yard, he started on Mrs. Honish.

"Do you still have that formal sofa?" I heard him ask. "You know that's not the right kind of sofa for a country house."

And I heard her laugh and say, "We're hoping to make it less country, Bo."

And him retort and God knows how much rum he had in him by this time, "That would be pretty hard to do."

"Well, you know," she said, "Mr. Honish was a plain man and liked what was around him to be plain, too." She sounded as if that included her and Pauline and that she was proud of it, but at the same time wasn't prepared for Bo to say, "Well, that certainly includes the two of you."

"Bo, I think you have had too much to drink," Mrs. Honish said then, "and that maybe Pauline and I better be going home."

As I emerged from the bathroom and saw Pauline slowly shifting, and she was slow in everything, and then sitting straight up in her chair, Bo said, loudly, "Do you know that old Mr. Honish always smelled like fertilizer?"

"Pauline," Mrs. Honish said, "honey, get up. We're going home."

"Go on," Bo yelled, then after a pause, shooting a mean look to the other side of the room, "You too, Essie."

Essie stood by the book case, cocktail glass in hand. "I'm enjoying it here," she said in her throaty voice, playing at being a short haired brunet Bacall. Her mother sat under the grape arbor on the patio just outside the room.

"Well," he said, "I am not enjoying you."

"Best bar in town," she told him, tilting her glass.

"You like bars, don't you, Essie? I remember Monterrey, how you liked bars there and," he paused, "bartenders." Bo later related how after he spurned her she took up with several.

"That'll do, Bo," she said, nodding toward the patio. "You see my mother is present."

"Well," he said, "she shouldn't still be here. She told me herself you both already had your supper. So why don't you and your conniving old mother go home?"

"I told you," she said, "I'm staying for the drinks."

"Come on, Pauline," Mrs. Honish said. But poor, overgrown Pauline seemed stuck to her chair. Bo turned toward Pauline then and said, "Your old Pa smelled like fertilizer." And then to Mrs. Honish. "Do you hear what I'm saying? Your whole family is a pile of shit."

"Bo!" Rena reprimanded as she poked her head in through the

breakfast room door, then turned and came through the living room toward me. I'd had one eye on this and at the front door had been listening. But was waving to Ben who was about to get out of the car.

"You hear all that?" she asked me. "I think it's disgusting."

"I don't know why he had them all here," I whispered. "He's never had any use for the Honishes and Miz Burnhardt has always irritated him and for that matter Miz Walsh." I spell the Miz out here so that you won't imagine I, in those days, said Ms. Miz Walsh was Robin Lee's mother. I thought it amazing that he hadn't done in Miz Walsh before she and Robin Lee took their lawn chairs outside by the flower bed where they sat nursing their drinks.

"He's just becoming mean. Just like Leeland."

"Aunt Rena," I said, "I don't get it."

"Honey," she told me, "he's drunk."

"Was he drunk when he invited them?" I asked. "Did he bring them here to insult them? Why not leave them alone?"

"If you ask me, he's drunk quite a lot lately," she told me. Then grinned at Ben who was upon us. She had always liked him. "Why hello, sweetheart."

"Oh," I said to her, not to Ben, giving Ben no explanation, "I'm glad I'm going."

Ben smiled back at her. By this time we were hand in hand on the porch. He said we were just going for a drive and then for something to eat in one of the drive-ins.

We didn't go there, though, but drove all the way to Padre. Nothing on it then. No hotels. Not even a hamburger stand. I still think of it like that.

I hear it's not so nice now. A lady I met recently on a train trip I took to and from Texas told me in no uncertain terms as we crossed West Texas desert what she thought of the state. "Don't judge all of Texas by the west of it," I told her. "It's different on the Gulf. I grew up in Corpus Christi."

"Oh," she said, "I hear that's tacky." Then she told me she had also heard Padre was full of expensive tourist traps. "Well," I retorted, "isn't everywhere?"

Surely nothing on it then. Just sand, all the way to Mexico. More than a hundred miles of sand against dark, sometimes threatening water. "Ben," I asked as he tore along over it, "just where do you think you are going?"

"Off the deep end maybe."

"Well, please don't take me, too."

He threw on the brakes then. "Listen," he said as he took me to him and I felt his trembling and felt my trembling, too. "Listen, I've got years of school ahead of me and I don't know how I'll make it—"

"I know that," I said to him.

"I don't want you to see anymore of whatever his name is."

"Dan," I told him.

"OK, I don't want you to see any more of Dan. The one with the cars."

Then his mouth was on my face, my throat, his thick lashes tickling the tip of my ear. "I don't want you to see him, you hear? I'll take you to those dumb parties."

One of the reasons I went with Dan to the parties sometimes was that I knew Ben made fun of them.

"No," I said and it was so hard to get words out that all I could do was whisper. "Leave me alone, let me go, take me back, now."

But even as I told him that, I clung close and let him kiss my face and run his hands over me; I tried to be still as he did it, early tried to train myself in stillness, but something inside me broke and before I realized what I was doing, I was all over him, too. With my hands, up his back and across his shoulders, with my mouth and voice, my beautiful radio voice, God only knows what I said.

And then he stopped and pushed me a little way from him. "Listen," he said, "Do you know why I'm like this? I'm nineteen years old and I have years of school ahead of me."

"You said that before and I know that," I told him.

"I don't know how we can be together. If I can ever marry you." I saw that he was in such dead earnest.

I turned from him and faced, instead, the window on what had been my side of the car.

"Ben," I said, "we shouldn't be here." I thought I saw a wind coming up and I knew the bridge without a fence wasn't safe. I remembered my mother's story of her and Bo and Rena and Leeland and the time they had all had of it in their little boat, then saw Ben and me in that boat and it sinking. "It's dangerous to be here," I told him. But Ben pulled me back to him and we stayed, kissing and caressing until the rain began to fall and maybe it was only that, the rain, that stopped us.

It seems in retrospect that at least in love, completion and fulfillment was prevented by something in the very elements down where we grew up.

Ben's hands were inside my blouse, on my breasts, then one was under my skirt on my thigh and after on the mound inside my panties; one of mine was on the shaft that was him where he had grown so hard; I wanted it and all of him still closer, but the car, by this time, was rocking, the rain slashing down in sheets. So we had to stop, but didn't until I said, in a rush, a whisper, what I had never said to anyone before. "Oh, I want you."

57

And he said, "I know it, but we're going to have to go."

By the time we got back on the mainland the fierce rain that had seemed to threaten flood had, unbelievably, stopped. In fact, on our side of you, Corpus, the ground was dry. As he drove I still cradled into one of Ben's arms.

When I got home I found Aunt Rena washing dishes in the kitchen and Bo slumped in a corner chair slurping coffee. I knew the coffee was to help him sober up. Grandma had been sleeping for awhile he said; he finally got her out on a combination of morphine and creme de menthe. "Grasshoppers," he told me, "I made a big pitcher. I finally got her out on those. She never knew there was any alcohol in them. 'Why, these,' she said, 'are so green and pretty. Bo you should have one of these instead of what you are drinking. The church teaches us that drinking alcoholic beverages is a sin.'" He looked up at me and grinned and didn't seem to care a bit that I was getting in at 1 a.m. "According to her preacher, that old frog faced bastard, anything that's any fun is a fucking sin."

We were both of us, Aunt Rena and I, taken back by the language.

"Bo, honey," Aunt Rena said, "why don't you just go on now to bed."

"I don't want to go to bed," Bo muttered, still leering at me. He didn't seem to care in the least where I had been.

Aunty sighed then and asked me if we had a nice ride and if in April I was going with Ben to the big senior dance at the Driscol.

I said we had driven all the way to Padre and back, I wanted to confess that much, and that just going and coming had taken a long time, but it was nice to do that once. I also said a wind with rain had come up over Padre, it scared me I said like I used to be scared by the thought of storm and being lost in the Gulf, floating, when we used to go to Ransom Island. I said, and I thought I was a convincing liar, that although we had planned to hunt for driftwood on Padre, we couldn't stay.

I also said I wasn't going to the dance at the Driscol in April, that by then I would have no time for dances.

"But, darlin'," Aunt Rena said, "you love dancing."

Later on in the Spring I told her that she was right and that I had changed my mind. But , still later, when it became clear to her that Dan, not Ben, was taking me, she said, "Yes, I see you are going, but would you tell me this? Why is it you are going with that radio boy instead of the good looking one with broad shoulders and wavy hair?"

And I said, "Ben talks of going steady and I don't want to get serious."

And she said, "Honey, if you go round with a boy who has shoulders like that, feel them against you, you'll never be serious, you'll just smile."

Part Two

Sayer, Oklahoma

I was remembering how Aunt Rena said that when I left Uncle Bo at the bus station this morning. I had to leave him there. I had been back in the middle of the country selling off things I'd had in storage ever since I worked for stations in Chicago and Omaha and later Kansas City, had possessions stored away in each of those cities, and was driving back now to the West Coast.

Tulsa was as far as Bo could come with me. Standing straight and taller than he's ever been, like a sapling that grows upright only as it gets older, Bo is now nearly through his seventies, his dark drinking years long over. I've needed his help in getting west where life and work have finally taken me, just as I needed it to go east when I was eighteen.

Until I came along, the Bells had never gone east, from the beginning had been caught up in western movement, so that what I'm doing late in my life seems finally right, the completion of some ancestor's longing or in my genes.

My mother's family were all Bells, my father's McElroys; my father, who took off long ago, had relatives in Boston and New York, which may explain my early longing for those places and certainly explains my coloring; except for Bo everyone else in the family was pale. "Dark Scot" Bo always said of my dark blue eyes and ashy hair. Ben told me once that my eyes were the darkest blue eyes he had ever seen, but at another time he told me they were slate grey and at still another, he concluded that they changed color with my moods or the weather.

My father, Burton McElroy, who, I was told, also had dark blue eyes, walked out on my mother and me when I was just a baby, he had gone a little crazy my mother said. Just took off one day in his old Studebaker, headed toward town, this was up near Nacogdoches, and never came back. Town was south of where we lived in the country and he went right through it and just kept driving that way.

"Poor Burt," my mother said, "he hardly knew what he was doing. He had been out of work, the Depression was on, you know, and your grandma had been at him. And besides that, he was grieving over the loss of his own people. Both his mother and father had died suddenly up north, within a few weeks of each other, and he didn't even have the fare to go back for their funerals. He'd had to live not only with, but off, the Bells, and Grandma, my mother said, began to make remarks about what he ate. So one day he just got in the Studebaker. "I don't think he really thought he was going much of anywhere."

And nobody knows how far he finally drove that car. In a dream I used to see him in the car and it in a body of water and fast sinking, waves breaking and water lapping against the windows. I always dreamed this dream at Aunt Rena's which was lucky because she was always there to hug and hold on to. "Oh, Aunt Rena," I would tell her, "I just had the most awful dream. Burton McElroy drove right off the coast of Texas. His car hadn't hugged the road right and was just swallowed up with him still in it by Corpus Christi Bay."

I think he must have died somewhere. He never wrote or sent money. After seven years my mother declared him dead in front of a lawyer who had helped her sign papers and then she married Bud whom she met when she first came to South Texas. Leeland, who was doing some building in Texas, wrote that the Depression hadn't struck the Texas coast the way it had the rest of the country, that Texas had money, that every little town wanted a music teacher.

I was just a baby when my mother left me with Grandma and Grandaddy. For a while Aunt Rena stayed with us in Arkansas and East Texas, too. Her family were all Brocks from Louisiana and there was talk of her being part Cajun and part black Creole and maybe she was. God knows her hair was black enough and her skin dark, her nose broad, though her eyes were merry and blue.

I thought of them as Santa Claus eyes because of the way they crinkled at the corners and because of the broad, almost chubby face they were set in.

Her full-lipped white-toothed smile seemed to me like Santa Claus, too.

As I write this Aunt Rena is—can you believe it?—still living, ninety-seven or ninety-eight, none of us knows for sure. I just sent her a birthday card, late by a month. We all keep forgetting Aunt Rena's birthday because it doesn't seem right she should still be having one. One way or another we all said good-bye years ago.

Nearly twenty years have gone by since she left East Texas to go back to Louisiana where she lives in a little house near one of her nephews. My mother always says, "Why in the world The Higher Power keeps Rena with us is hard to say."

Except for Bo and my mother all my other kinfolk have departed. Now here I am in middle life, past my middle forties, leaving the country that nurtured all of us, that is, generally the southwestern middle of it, which includes a sprawl.

Tulsa this morning seemed to me such a plain, concrete city and, as it appeared downtown anyway, completely utilitarian, without flowering tree or bush. Maybe I noticed because of the contrast to the hilly and flowery streets of Los Angeles. Or, maybe it's just that August in the hot middle with prairie stretching out on every side spares so little.

When I'm in L.A. I miss the prairie; it steadied me to know that in every direction that I could see I faced a sweep of land. And to my surprise, when I first saw the Pacific sorrow welled up in me.

Bo certainly hadn't favored my trip toward it. He wanted me near, wanted me in some near city: Dallas, Houston, New Orleans. Even Tulsa seemed reachable enough. But when he finally understood that L. A. was the only city with a job I wanted, he helped. Helped me pack up the few pieces of light furniture I had decided to keep and to sell the rest. Now from Tulsa a Houston bound bus would take him through to Texarkana and then into the East Texas woods and home.

In the bus station he grumbled about the coffee. "It's like water," he said, "and in such an ugly mug."

"I don't think it's bad," I told him.

"I like good strong coffee. And in a china cup. I guess I shouldn't be in a bus station."

I felt bad that I didn't have the money to buy him a plane ticket. He was even paying his own bus fare. For years Bo worked in insurance so he would have some, and I had never worked a job that didn't pay.

He told me then that his life hadn't come to much.

"Oh," I said, "you were a super salesman after you got out of that insurance job you hated." After his breakdown he got a job in Foley's department store, selling housewares at first and, later, designer dresses. Then I added, "And for all of us, you made so many houses home." Even more important I wanted to tell him, but didn't, he wove a magic web of fantasy through them, in room after room talking out with me and sometimes with my friends and with Old Spanish his and our dreams.

In spite of his white hair and light eyes and his timidity, plus what was in my mind, a cruel German-English way or two, Bo was the exotic of the family, his skin as dark as mine.

"Uncle Bo," I wanted to tell him, "we are black Scots together." I sometimes thought, of course, that my darkness came from my family's other side. The unknown side, swallowed in my dream by Corpus Christi Bay and the Gulf of Mexico. And that may be.

"You made so many houses home." Right after I said that he reminded me of the state asylum.

"I remember the morning they came and took me away and locked me up," he told me. "I remember Bud signing the papers that sent me to Austin." That his own family had locked him up, that was the part he couldn't get over. "Oh what did I do? What did I do? I wondered."

"Hey," I said, "that's over. You did a lot." I was sorry we had gotten off on all this and wanted to change the subject. "You gave all my friends such good times when they came to visit."

"Good old Uncle Bo makes a mean martini." He took a big gulp of coffee. "And drinks a bunch of them."

"Why don't you stop coming down on yourself?" I asked him.

He just went on slurping. "So this is Tulsa. What a dead town."

"It's six o'clock in the morning," I said. "I expect it will liven up."

"Well," he went on, "I don't think I did much. 'Not worth killing.' That's what my keeper said. Said I shook a knife at Bud or somebody, I don't remember. I couldn't have shaken a knife at your mother could I? Couldn't have shaken a knife at Leona?"

After a pause he said, "But a drunk will do anything. And doesn't know anything. Never recalls anything. I had been blind with blackout. I remember them saying I shook a knife at somebody. They talked about it just before they took me away. I seem to remember Leona saying, 'Officer, he didn't mean to do it. He didn't go to do it.' And I remember the fuss they had about me, Bud and your mother. I guess that fuss helped split them up. I remember your Aunt Rena saying, your good-for-nothing Aunt Rena, 'He hurts himself mostly.'"

I tried to tune him out. I hated this review, hated his self pity, most of all hated what he said about Aunt Rena. I could hear her saying, could hear her so clearly, "That's what we all do, hurt ourselves when we hurt each other. But we can't seem to help it and it just goes on and on."

Later

Jay had come to our house on Palm Drive one scorching afternoon when it was nearly a hundred degrees. And sticky. We had all stripped down to practically nothing, Bo just home from work, barefoot and shirtless in a pair of old paint pants, my mother in a gauzy skirt and halter top—she had a half dozen of them in neutral colors made every summer—me in tattered shorts and a bathing suit top, all of us dripping sweat.

Bo was embarrassed for us. "Well, here we all are nearly naked," he said. "When I got home I just stripped down."

In seersucker pants and sport shirt, his waiter's jacket with a tie in the pocket over one arm, Jay was obviously dressed for work. Not that he seemed to mind; he was grinning. Said, "I can take the bedroom. I told Frank I wanted it, that I needed my own place." Bo looked pleased and Jay couldn't hide his happiness. "Of course I'll pay you for it," he said. "Just like a regular roomer."

Then a surprising thing happened. In what I have come to think of as his "for the public" voice and by this I guess I mean the less sincere one, the voice he puts on when he's trying to protect himself, Bo said, "Why, Jay, we'll be glad to have you and don't worry about any money." But he couldn't have sounded colder if he had told Jay never to darken our door.

Then Jay said again, but this time stammering, that he would pay.

The four of us stood in a circle there on the sunporch staring at one another, sweat dripping. In those days we didn't have air-conditioning, only fans. My mother and Bo and I all popped up from our seats when Jay first came in. Jay's pale shirt was ringed in front with sweat, exposing a nipple.

"Sit down with us," my mother said. "We have cold cuts and potato salad. Have you time for a bite of supper?"

"Oh, n-n no m-m-mam," Jay stuttered.

"Well, maybe you'd like some tea. Just before she left Rena made a big cold pitcher." Aunt Rena was once again at the movies or so she said. I thought she was smart to so often opt for air-conditioning. In the last three weeks she claimed to have seen every show in town.

"She visits nasty old men in their rooming houses," I could hear my grandmother say. Grandma thought the whole human race was "nasty." But I felt sure Aunt Rena visited no one with whom she had not first gone to the movies or at least no one with whom she had not discussed going to the movies, on a bus or in one of the city parks.

"M'-m-maybe I w-w-ill—" Jay stopped there, just couldn't get it all out. "Maybe I will have some tea." But then, after a pause, said without a bit of trouble that he expected the restaurant to have quite a business since it was Friday night and a hot one, cooler at Las Hadas than in most people's houses. By this time he was grinning like a school kid at my mother. He told Bo then that the room was going to be good to do his work in and that he hoped it would be all right to bring his drawing board and little drawing table and maybe, even an easel. "I-l-l-ff I u-u-se o-o-oil p-p-paint I I I-'ll t-t-take th-th-them o-o-outside."

"It'll be fine for you to do anything you like in the room," Bo said in his phoney voice, smiling his false smile. "It'll be just fine, "he said. But he looked uneasy.

Bo was, I knew, pleased that Jay was with us and had accepted his offer of the room. But I could also tell that it was not going to be all right for Jay to do anything he liked in it, and this did strike me as an odd turn of events, and possibly it was not going to be all right for him to be in it at all.

Was this because the room had been Grandma's I wondered or because Bo had begun to have certain fears?

"I think it will be nice to have Jay," I told Bo later. We were in the room adding splotches of color; at Litchenstein's we had bought a bedspread, tailored and navy blue, but with a small geometrical gold colored design.

"Do you think it's nice?" Bo seemed to want my honest opinion.

"I do," I told him. And I did. I looked forward to having someone near my age at home, someone like a big brother. I had felt that close to Jay from the start.

"Well, then," Bo said, "I do, too."

But by the next night when he came home from his office he didn't think so.

In the office he had blurted out his news to both Pauline Honish, who, in case I haven't told you, also worked there answering phones, and Essie Burnhardt and by the end of the day, his boss had called him in for a talk. From what I could make of what Bo said, the talk was about grief, about what happens to people when they grieve.

"'You, don't know what you are doing, Bo, you have just lost your mother. That's what the old bastard told me.

"'You don't know that boy really. Where does he come from? Who are his people?'

"'They live out west somewhere,' I told him. 'He still has a sister out there; his mother and father have both passed away.'

"'Well, the S.O.B. said, 'but—'

"'You think he is odd, why don't you say it? You think he's queer.' I used that word, just blurted it out; you should have seen his face, the old bastard. 'You think I'm queer?'

"'Why no, I don't think you know what you are doing.'"

"I wish I could have told him off, wish I could have walked out right there."

Bo often said the happiest day of his life would be the day he could walk out of that office. But I don't think that's the way things turned out. His last day there was the one before Bud, who had been in town just a few days himself, took him off to Austin. So it wasn't so much that he walked out of the office as that he walked into a nuthouse and a jail.

But he put the Palm Drive house on the market shortly after the day when he came home upset and mad from the reprimands he had gotten at the office. I was sorry we wouldn't have Jay with us, but I knew there were better places to live in you, Corpus. And I could hardly stand our neighbors, Lana's family, although Lana had been my friend.

Still later in Sayer

I had felt sorry for Lana; she hated the way she looked which explains why she bleached her hair and then combed it in that silly peek-a-boo style which hid her but blinded her, too. And I hated the neighborhood where we all lived. Lana also hated it, and I knew her family never helped her feel better about anything. I thought it was pathetic that, afraid as she was, she still tried so hard to be sexy.

One day a few weeks after Jay had started visiting, Lana's brother came over to ask me what kind of place we thought we were running; he said he wasn't sure he wanted his mother and sister living next door.

It has taken me forever to learn anything and I didn't get all the implications of his questions; I had only the vaguest notion about what caused him to ask them. Nevertheless, I felt something for him that I can only describe as being close to loathing and I said, "Get out. Get out of our yard."

"Don't you understand anything?" I asked as he bore a hole through me, by just looking. "I want you out of here so GET. And don't ever come back again." Then I added, "Tell your mother to stay out, too."

I stopped at that. I couldn't bring myself to exclude Lana who was one of my first Corpus Christi friends. She always aimed to please and she had been so lonely. I reasoned she couldn't help who she was related to.

Brad looked me up and down the way he had seen some actor in a grade B movie do, fixing his attention finally on the crotch of my lime green shorts. He said, "You know what you need, don't you?"

I couldn't answer, only stiffened and clinched my fist, ground my teeth, pressed my thumbs against the backside of my knuckles hard.

"That's Elizabeth McElroy," Gerry told me years later. "Like her mother, a teeth-grinding fist-maker." But I only remember making those gestures once, on that day I ordered Brad out of the yard.

Brad grinned at me and mumbled, "Maybe someone ought to give it to you."

"I get along all right by myself," I told him.

"You're the kind of nut it's best to stay away from," he said. "And you might as well know it now, no regular guy in town is ever going to go out with you."

His tone of voice let me know he would see to that. "You never even comb your hair," he said, looking this time at my cowlicks, "and you live with a— " He stopped. Then said, "You're always going to be stuck with some Spic-queer—or a Jew."

I let go then and began to pound him, his chest and then his face, then with bare grass-stained feet kicked him in the shins and then the groin. I don't know what would have happened, how badly he might have hurt me, he had his hands on my throat, if Bo hadn't come out on the patio, slamming the door to the sunporch behind him. Brad let go of me fast then and ducked under the pink gate which I immediately locked.

"Nut," he yelled back over one shoulder. And then, and this was directed at Uncle Bo, "Queer."

Bo called the realtor that very afternoon. "Nice friends you have, Elizabeth," he told me.

"He's no friend of mine," I said, "he's just Lana's brother."

"Un huh, I see," Bo said, "nice boy."

When Jay came over later, bringing some of his things, Bo said he would have to make other arrangements, that he was sorry and that of course he should have told Jay he was going to do it, but he had just put the house on the market. "I'm sorry, but I can't stay here any longer. For now you'll have to go back to Frank's."

Jay stood on one foot, then the other and looked down at them. When he finally raised his head I saw his pain and I don't think I've ever again seen such a look of disappointment on anybody's face.

Betrayal, I was sure that was the word he would say.

But he didn't. He just stood without speaking on the front porch, still purple with bougainvillea, where Bo had made his pronouncement. I watched his whole body sink: knees, chest, shoulders.

Before this terrible sadness a knot in my own chest tightened. I still feel the weight of it from time to time. And without saying anything, all caved in like that, Jay turned to go.

And Bo didn't call after him.

As far as I know he never apologized or ever offered more in the way of explanation.

After Jay left, Bo high-tailed it to Robin Lee's.

And still later

But didn't get there what he had counted on. Unconditional love. Or, at least, sympathy. Not the way he told it.

"What she said to me was, 'Bo, you might as well know this. I've heard some things about you. People think that Jay, that there's something the matter with him. Not just his stuttering. Something that maybe causes his stuttering. Now, you understand, I'm not saying this. I'm just telling you about people.' Can you believe she would say this to me? When I told her I had no idea what she was talking about she looked at me and said things that were even stranger."

"'Bo, I'm going to be thirty-four years old,'" she said. 'You're a lot older.'" Bo was forty-eight. "'I think some things between you and me should soon be settled.' 'What things?' I asked her. 'You know how I feel about you. Why, we're close. Close friends.'"

"Then she told me, 'I think you know what I'm saying.'"

"Listen, a lot has happened to me," I told her. "I have let a lot hit me, and a whole lot has been taken. Can't you see that? My life's just a blank now."

"She said it wouldn't have to be a blank, that it could be nice, that I could fill it."

He stopped for a second, then said, "What I'm trying to get across to you, Elizabeth, is that in the late fall—" He cleared his throat. "Around Thanksgiving I've agreed to marry Robin Lee."

Then, over just a couple of ice cubes, he filled a water glass to the top with bourbon.

"If you want to drink," he told me once, "and live to any age at all after you begin to do it, buy and drink only the highest quality bourbon. Scotch has a nasty foreign taste, so forget it. And never drink any kind of rot gut. Or vodka which rots holes in your brain and makes you crazy. Or killer gin."

Still in Sayer

Certain times in life for certain places. I'm pointed west now though who knows if I'll stay or for how long. I'm not sure I'll see my Uncle Bo much more. He's talked for years about making a return to the Gulf Coast although I don't know now that he can go. He says he hates the pine woods more than ever. He never liked them. He says, "I want out into open country. I hate living in all that dark."

"Maybe I'll go to Galveston," he told me just this morning. As I drove on and all the way across Oklahoma I remember him saying that. And here in this motel where I rest and write this and drink even more bad coffee, I watch on the TV that hangs over the counter the big hurricane Alicia wash over that town.

Wash over the old Galvez Hotel where we ate several holiday dinners and which has long lived on in my mind as a reminder of Bo and Grandma and all the family and what I sometimes falsely think of as gentler and better times.

They weren't, all things considered.

Now I see the Galvez is all but gone. And I know that when Bo sees the waves wash over it, he will by this time probably be home to see it on his own TV, his dreams about returning will be gone too.

Each year he has fantasized about returning to a different Gulf Coast town, all but you, Corpus Christi—Rockport, Port Lavaca, Aransas Pass, Port Isabel. But, I suspect, Galveston was the town he thought he really might get to.

Once Uncle Bo drove my mother and Rena and Grandma and me to Galveston just so we could eat Thanksgiving dinner. I had been there for the first time with Uncle Leeland when he and his crew were building bridges, rode the bus from Livingston on a highway called "The Hug the Coast."

From where I lay stretched out on the back seat, the three grown-ups crammed together in front, I was only aware of fat clouds and blue sky. The road when I saw it was only a shiny little sliver of a thing, clean and empty. Oh, I often think, that was the time for traveling in Texas!

Because I got car sick I always had the backseat all to myself. Bo or my mother always spread a pallet for me there and put a bucket of cokes and ice and cut limes and a pan with a washrag in it, for me to throw up in, on the floor. The coke and lime never prevented my car sickness as everyone hoped it might. But that I got car sick also never stopped us from going anywhere. Or stopped me from wanting to.

Very early that Thanksgiving morning, and it was still years from the Thanksgiving that was first scheduled to be Bo's wedding day, Bo said he would drive us all to Galveston. Grandma and Aunty had been grumbling over coffee about making dressing and about the, for them, dismal prospects of cooking a turkey all day; they had already, at eight in the morning, set the pecan and pumpkin pies out to cool.

"I would rather go to the Galvez and have crab," Bo said, "and have those pies when we come home. Who needs turkey and dressing?"

"Well, I don't know about going all the way to Galveston," my mother said, nervous, expectant, laughing, dutifully pointing out that Galveston was two hundred miles away; everyone in the family expected my mother to be practical as if to compensate for Bo.

Bo said your hotels wouldn't serve crab, Corpus, that you were in your ways, if not in your population, too small-town. Anyway, he said we should have a change of scene.

"I like turkey," Aunt Rena said (Aunt Rena liked everything), "but it would be fun to go."

"Well, then," Grandma said, "I expect the Galvez has turkey, too."

I knew then we would get off.

On our way out of town we gave our uncooked turkey to the Gonzales family who lived on the corner and who often sent us homemade tamales at Easter and during Christmas time.

Now here I am in this sad looking little town, its houses sagging in the heat, just a few miles from the Texas Panhandle, not too far from Amarillo, before I leave my Motel 6 looking at Galveston in black and white in all that strange weather. Strange weather all over the world, the Doomsday folk tell us, as they always have. But we see it, shadowlike, in more places, see a big hurricane named Alicia now washing the old Galvez away.

"Maybe Galveston's too big," Bo said to me just this morning when he talked of wanting to get back to the coast. "And once in a while," he went on, "it freezes. If we moved south far enough we would never get cold. Port Isabel or even Port Lavaca might be better. Port Isabel is the southern most point in the United States."

Bo never mentions you, Corpus Christi. After he came back from the crazy-house, he had to live in you with shame.

By the time he had to face you, Jay had taken off and Robin Lee's mother had moved Robin Lee to her relatives who lived near San Antonio.

Bo broke their engagement the first time three days before Thanksgiving and broke it the second time, the following June, just hours before he was scheduled to show up at the First Methodist church.

Although Robin Lee finally came back to you, Corpus, people tell us she was never the same, was someone entirely different, much older, prettier, and surer of herself, but super serious and sick quite a lot.

As soon as he could, Bo left for Houston where Jay helped him get a job with Foley's; at first he handled designer clothes for women, after working in housewares for a time, and later became the buyer for designer clothes for both women and men.

And after my mother's marriage to Bud broke up, my mother joined him and began her own business, a music store. The two of them were in their own way, happy. What they knew about mostly was work and in those days Houston was a good town to work and work hard in. Bo said it was always against his better judgment and my mother's too, to retire near Aunt Rena in the pines.

"I may not be around too much longer," he said this morning when I put him on the bus. And I, thinking of Aunt Rena, way up in her nineties, was put out with him.

"Oh, you don't know," I told him. Bo is only seventy-five, not old in our family.

"I have premonitions," he told me. "God gives us premonitions."

Aunt Rena always called them signs.

Near New Mexico
Near Santa Rosa

Signs all right on old route 66, now Interstate 40, on the road to California. Near the end of Oklahoma, just the other side of Sayer where I last wrote, I pulled off early to stretch and have some coffee, hardly able to deal with contemplating the miles I have to go, then afterwards came straight across the Panhandle and into New Mexico on good, straight roads, the wind behind me and hours still ahead with light.

As I drove I cried for Bo. And also thought sadly of Aunt Rena. When I last talked to her on the phone her voice was so clear. Until just last spring she got around all right, every spring planted a flower garden and some beloved vegetables, too. She always cooked and ate a lot of them. But she can't navigate anymore and when she tries, just topples over. Seems cruel to me because Rena loved to travel, was off to Acapulco on Uncle Leeland's insurance money just a few days after he was in the ground. You can imagine what Grandma said. If she couldn't take a big trip, she would take a little one, if only on one of the city buses.

"Rena, where do you go on the bus?" Grandma always asked her.

"Why," she would answer, "to the picture shows. Or sometimes just downtown to bum through Kress's, you know I always did love to Kress a little, or sometimes," she laughed, "I'll just ride to the end of the line. I always meet somebody. Somebody who likes a good time." And Grandma's lip would curl up at Rena.

Later I would hear her talking about Aunt Rena as if she were a whore. And would see when I looked at Aunt Rena that she had been crying.

And sometimes I just let Grandma have it. "Talk that way about Aunt Rena if you want," I would tell her, "but don't let her hear you and hold your tongue in front of my friends."

When C.C. came over and heard some of the things Grandma said, I was embarrassed to be related. I was also mortified the night Grandma convinced my mother to have C.C. and I followed. They thought we were going somewhere to be with boys; we were just on our way out in the country to see Gerry when I caught sight, in our rear view mirror, and this was in T.J.'s car, of Mother and Bud behind us. C.C. had been telling me of her troubles with Travis and how she hoped he would get away, but to college, not to the army. Talk of war was all around us. "Oh," she said, "I hate it when he says he is going to enlist."

We were a family, and finally a town, of travelers.

How many places I had been with Uncle Bo.

Dear Uncle Bo, (I said on the card I just wrote.)

I have missed your company. We have taken a lot of trips together and today I have remembered them all.

Then I made a remark about the scenery and the weather, so much cooler than the weather we had been in back there, and then I wrote that I loved him. I had never done that before.

It seems right to me now that I think back on it that we left each other in the early morning hours, him going back on the bus to a place where the light is paler, me driving straight into it out of a hot wind.
"Here we are, two single people," Bo had said back in the bus station, just before he boarded. I thought maybe it was the last time we would see each other. In a flash then I saw Robin Lee and Jay, saw their faces, Robin Lee's wry smile, Jay's broad one and also saw for just a minute the faces of the two young men who had, for any period of time been in my life, both Easterners, the first of whom made me feel I ought to shuck my background, conceal my identity or change it. "Sometimes Elizabeth," he would often reprimand me, "I can't imagine where you grew up." He was an opera lover, what we had in common: a love for opera, a pale-skinned, blue-eyed Philadelphian, now an announcer for QXR. The other, a jazz fan more tolerant of my origins, but so different from me, had grown up in the Bronx. I hadn't lived under a roof with either of them. This doesn't seem the right place for me to tell you about them and, maybe, there is none. But Bo and I once had both considered sharing our lives with these others. I could hear Aunt Rena saying, "He could have lived with a person outside his family if he had wanted to."
Could he or I have done that? I remember asking Joe if happiness is important, I thought he surely had the answer to life's big questions, and I can still hear the resonance of his impassioned, "Yes."

"I was never afraid of work, hard work," I could hear Grandaddy saying. Well, none of his children were either, and certainly Grandma wasn't , though they were afraid of other things.
"Mother," Leeland always said to Grandma, "for God's sake hire some help. You're killing yourself with so much housework, cooking and canning on that wood stove, then sewing all afternoon into the night." And I can hear Grandma telling him, "Whoever I hired wouldn't clean to suit me, would just piddle around." Bo locked himself in the room with her that hot June day she died and wasn't sober for long periods after. I guess I have already told you a lot about that summer, how sometimes he would sober up for Jay or Robin Lee. But he didn't stay sober until after he was released from the asylum. He went berserk in the fall after he had

taken me to college; after he was released he never drank again, but he also didn't laugh much or spin out his dreams.

Bo spent nearly a year in the state hospital and was visited often, or so he told me, by a beautiful girl from what was then the ward for "nymphs." He considered bringing her home he said, but she overdosed before they released her; he told me this story many times and told me other sad ones.

When asked, he assisted with shock treatments and lobotomies.

When he finally came home to the cream colored house where he had moved us—the house was close to the street and practically downtown, all of us sitting on the porch he had painted shrimp pink—the first person he talked to was Robin Lee.

I thought I had never seen her look so pretty. She was wearing, in complementary contrast to our loud porch, a sleeveless linen dress in robin's egg blue, the color that matched her name. Her hair, which when not in a pony tail or in pigtails usually hung limply around her shoulders, was done in a French roll. She seemed to me, and I expect to Bo, too, many years older. And so much calmer.

But then, how must he have seemed to her? To me he was almost a stranger; it had been so many years since I had been with him when he was really sober. He seemed all flattened out.

"You're looking well, Bo," she told him. His smile was faint; he took her hands and said, "You, too." (She died of bronchitis a few weeks after.)

She was all composure when she said, "I thought about you." He told her then in a matter of fact way that he had thought about her, too. I wondered if he had much. As he talked, my mother and I pumped on the porch swing.

"Everyone hopes you will come back to the office," she told him. Then she was quiet for a second; he didn't speak. "Maybe you have heard I have been out of town."

"People in my family," I told Joe Copeland, "people in my family don't just drink too much and then have genteel breakdowns from which they recover in fashionable sanitariums. And after that take crusies. They get locked up in jails or crazy houses. Or fall out of hospital windows." Uncle Leeland had almost done that when he was in the hospital to dry out, two big nurses and a nun pulled him from the ledge.

Later he claimed he was jumping because he had to get away from the nun. "Meanest woman," he told me, "God ever put breath in."

"Darling," Joe said, "we are alike. The people in my family, too."

Santa Monica
From my new apartment nearer the station.

That we were alike, of course, was exactly what I wanted him to tell me.

He told me stories of alcoholic uncles, desire-ridden aunts, explosive fathers, or shiftless ones, of mothers who were nagging and martyred or sex-starved and restless, of crazy people, mothers and fathers, uncles and aunts, who ran away from their children and each other and of all the children he knew who were abandoned or who died of horrible diseases or, worse sometimes, who lived on with broken hearts.

He laughed before he said, "I wanted to tell some good news. Something exciting. Wanted to play some music, put on some drama. Build a network. Something for us all."

We were alike and I had wanted him to tell me.

One way in which we weren't alike, he had married, had made a household, or rather, households, had apartments in London and New York, while I traveled precariously through the world, all my stars in air signs in spite of my New Year's birth.

Once again I was trying to relocate. No job with any station seemed to last. I wanted work in a place that would put on my dramas. That meant, with Joe's help, and I was grateful for it, National Public Radio and very little money. Probably even meant working another job.

I guess nobody talks anymore about making any move final, but I thought I might stay in Los Angeles three to five years. I had been grieving prematurely over Bo when I lost Joe. I see that now.

Like Leeland on the ledge, my people hang on even when there's not much to hang on to.

I had idolized Joe and followed his career since childhood. Seemed to me sometimes that I had always known him, that I had no life before him. I met him the year I graduated from you, C.C. I told you that, and in the fabric of my life that memory is one of the brightest colors. But we didn't meet again until just a few years ago at Dan's station, KSD in Dallas and later at WKY in Oklahoma City.

At first he barely remembered me. Wouldn't have if I hadn't been Leona Bell's daughter, oh, he remembered my mother!

He had, even then, a fatal illness. And I grieved for Bo. And slipped away when I wasn't looking, his heart just failed, as if he had planned it, as if being free of his body was what he wanted.

I read somewhere that you can hold people to their bodies, to relationships, to desire, by prayer. The piece quoted a dying man who asked his wife to stop praying so that he could get on with what he was doing.

"Damn you," it reported him saying, "stop your selfish praying," and that shocked her so that she stopped. And with the energy she transmitted through prayer gone, he took a last breath.

By the time I met him at Dan's station, Joe was in a body that no longer made a good home. Twice Joe gave me just the boost I needed, and was about to give me so much more, but he couldn't stick around.

And in that regard was like Julia Winter, my English teacher at Corpus Christi High School who along with our famous Miss V, oh, V for Victory, launched me on my creative life.

My religious life. With so much energy going out over the airways, radio did one of the jobs of prayer, connected my mother to Miss V and Miss Winter to me. Life to life to life.

Before I met Joe, before I won that contest, Miss Winter encouraged me to go east to college and late in September of 1952 Bo and I climbed in the DeSoto and took off.

Except for Miss V, Miss Winter was my most important teacher and edited my first scripts.

Miss Winter taught an honors course in dramatic writing which she had a chance to begin because we had one of the first radio stations in the state. I almost didn't take it because I couldn't take everything and I thought a course in shorthand might be of more practical use.

But I adored Miss Winter, as I later did Joe, and months before I broke down and took her course, asked her to edit my contest entry.

I still remember some of our conversations.

"You see," I remember saying to her and remember being surprised she didn't laugh, "you see, I hear voices." Miss V who had more professional savvy and who was much more worldly, would have made a joke. "I put down what they tell me," I went on, "and what they call out to each other. And when they stop, I stop, but sometimes, when I rearrange what they tell me, I have a radio play. I've written one the station here will put on and I think I might get it on in other places."

"And so you might," she said, "but I'll bet that's not the reason you wrote it."

I didn't answer.

C.C. told me once it was plain I loved Miss Winter, that Ben was the only other person at the high school she had seen me look at just that way. I wondered if it was the same way she looked at Travis, the way Bo looked at Jay. As often as not when I was outside her classroom talking to Miss Winter, I could see C.C. and Travis making out in front of the door to the art room which was just down at the end of the hall. Wherever they were they nibbled at each other. C.C. could draw better than anybody at the school, but Travis was almost as good and getting better and better.

Oh all this, this memory, is just a few weeks before Travis left, split from you and from C.C., Corpus, and with that other girl.

"Even if I can't produce the script, I mean commercially," I told Miss Winter, "it may help me get a radio job. CHSR is going to put it on." CHSR stood for Corpus Christi High School Radio.

In the kindest possible way Miss Winter told me she thought I should get a general education.

"Well," I said, "I don't know what I would do with that." A major in speech and communications would, I was sure, get me a job in radio, if not in writing and producing my own drama or in interviewing and reviewing—and even then, these possibilities seemed to me fanciful—in programming or instruction, in the business end.

"Have you thought of television?" Miss Winter asked me. "Does Miss Van De Meyer encourage you in that?"

Miss V hadn't. I don't think she knew much about it. Who did? Until my first year in college no one I knew had a set.

But Miss V knew all right about radio, had been a programmer for several Texas stations, did broadcasting when she was in the navy.

She had also done some parachuting in the navy and her chute failed once in California, over a field at the edge of an orchard so that she came down in a Japanese pear tree. She still limped from the fall.

"That's what she gets," I heard, and she heard, people say, "for acting like a man." Even navy personnel, her superior and others, she told me once, had made remarks like that.

Although neither Miss V nor Miss Winter had been married, many seemed to believe that Miss Winter's single state went along with her being a school teacher, an occupation that she somehow had to adopt and a second best thing. Best, of course, would have been the occupations of wife and mother. Talk had it that her fiance was killed early in the war.

On the other hand, most people thought Miss V's singleness was unnatural and went along with some kind of perversion though nobody would explicitly say what. She could not have been accused of being thick with women for there were none, either old or young, around her. Her students revered and loved her but kept their distances and everyone knew were just her students, though some also became her friends.

Alone, into herself, unnatural, no wonder she limps, has a sickness. That was as much as I heard anybody whisper. Or, sometimes, just say.

"No," I said to Miss Winter. "I don't think she knows much about television. And I've hardly seen any. What I really care about is sound, working in sound. I think I could make a little money at it. Enough at least to live."

They laughed at me in Hollywood when I said all I wanted was to make a living. Except for the people at KCRW everyone I meet thinks I should learn to write for TV or the screen.

But I don't. I write to you about Miss Winter and Miss V.

Younger than Miss Winter, Miss V was blonde and scrubbed looking with pink cheeks and bright blue eyes, and like mine, fine, unruly hair. No one ever imagined a lover for her or connected her in any way with romance, though of the two women she had led by far the most dramatic life.

Tall and willowy, Miss Winter combed her hair away from her face and always wore a flower, often a red hibiscus or a bright rose behind one ear. Thin skinned and lightly freckled with a small overbite and slightly protruding teeth, she was sparkly-eyed, would have been beautiful, Lana said, if she had worn her hair loose around her shoulders.

"She brushes it back to show off her wit," I said, one could tell she had it, "so nothing will show but her mind."

But no matter what I said, her shiny brown hair was noticeable, maybe because she stuck those flowers in it, and C.C. said she thought Miss Winter meant it to be.

Back then, and this was before I met Joe, I thought Miss Winter had the answers to life's most important questions and I was in earnest when I asked what she thought I might do with a "general" education.

She said, "Why, learn from it, Elizabeth, and enjoy!"

"You don't understand," I told her. "Everyone in my family works. Always have." Even the married women, I wanted to tell her. What I had said was, I thought, the central truth about us. And that Julia Winter would surely understand.

Aunt Rena was, of course, outside blood-ties. Grandma always said Aunt Rena had no ambition, didn't care how poor she was. Once I heard a group of distant cousins, Grandma's nieces and great nieces whispering about Aunt Rena's origins. Was Aunt Rena of another race I wondered. And if she was, how did that make her different?

Were other races more inclined toward different ways of living? Were they more loving? I didn't know.

All I knew was that Aunt Rena had married into a family who worked and who respected work most when it brought in money. My grandmother whipped up dresses, my mother taught music and both were paid. No one thought much of Uncle Leeland when he just stayed home drinking and drawing up plans for buildings that no one had commissioned.

I also knew Aunt Rena had married into a family that had a streak of cruelty in it. We were, I knew, cruel to ourselves and sometimes to one another, perhaps because we repressed our impulses toward loving.

"A regular work house," Rena would often say. "It tires me out just to be around you people."

"Well, Elizabeth," I can still hear Julia Winter saying, "I'm going to place my hard earned money on what I'm going to tell you. And that is, that no matter what kind of education you get, general or otherwise, you will work, too."

Then she asked me if I wanted to live and be old and that surprised me and still does. She wasn't sick then. I said of course I did, yes.

"So do I," she told me, her eyes crinkling at the corners, a devilish glint in her crooked smile. "Oh I do, too."

On the Sunset Limited
Southern Pacific, Austin bound

But she didn't live and I lost her. The following winter she got the flu, then bronchial pneumonia, then leukemia; she died during the first spring I was away in school.

Grieving goes on for so long. I think it was Julia Winter I was, when I last wrote, telling you about.

Who would have thought that nearly a year would pass between letters and that when I wrote again I would, with engagements in three cities, be bound for Texas's heart? We have just pulled out of El Paso, Phoenix and Tucson far behind. I have always liked crossing the country by train, and I like working on it, watching the landscape slowly change from one kind to a totally different other. And in this part of my life I seem fated to swing back and forth between the far west and the middle of the country, just as when I was young I did between the middle of the country and New York.

When people asked me where I was from I used to say "I'm a Texan." Now I say, "I have lived in a lot of places." And I'm always homesick and yet no matter how many times I return, never feel I have arrived at home.

Hell, I had told Travis, I want to get out of Hell.

The chartered bus I rode to Dallas after I won the radio drama contest took me almost out. I had just turned sixteen. A bunch of students who wanted to tour the Big-D stations and meet important performers, announcers and programmers rode with me. We were all excited and it was March and spring.

The days had begun to turn warm in you, Corpus, leaves coming out on the trees in sticky green buds. And the Gulf had begun to sing. Far across town as we lived from it, I seemed to wake each morning to its singing.

The feel of the sun through the bus window told me that soon I would wear only cotton, that in another month I would be in sun dresses of soft colors. That year I favored lavender, maybe because it is a fantasy shade and that was a time for dreams. On the bus I saw shiny lavender cloth before me, smelled it, the polished cotton. I took such pleasure in smells and inhaled all the ones I had cared particularly for, all the new leaves and new cotton and linen and the straw of new hats.

I remembered a straw cloche with a bunch of cloth violets pinned to one side, a hat Grandma and I decorated together before the onset of her illness, her last healthy spring on Earth and before she got so cranky, though she always had a little something critical to say. "It's a good thing this is a cloche and close fitting," she told me. "It may once and for all tame that wild head of hair your father gave you, stick those cowlicks down to your head."

Bumping over the Texas countryside on that bus I wore the prim grey suit she had made me. Slate grey, she called it. Ben said that in rainy weather or when I was sad it was the color of my eyes. Back then if we were really going somewhere, we dressed up, wouldn't have dreamed of arriving in jeans, jeans were for hayrides and Saturday mornings.

On the bus I was careful of the way I sat because I didn't want to wrinkle my skirt and through all the miles was expectant, excited, looking out the windows at the new grass and all that rolling country and at the delicate little field flowers that had appeared suddenly. Some, like the bluebonnet when we came on a whole expanse of them, took my breath; they made a flag of a field, a flag that stretched out as far as I could see.

"When you are really yourself, Elizabeth," Ben told me after giving me a bunch of bluebonnets he had picked in the vacant lot, "your eyes aren't grey at all, they're darkest blue." Just before I left on this trip I took the flowers out of the vase on my desk where I had stuck them and into the bathroom where I held them against my face as I looked into the mirror, the only one in the house except for those in Grandma's room, to see if what Ben said was true.

Which brings me to a thought. Some postures are, maybe, for each of us, characteristic. Here I am still traveling. Looking out a window. At a desert this time and in August, too.

Much farther east the fields are all burnt up, but in six or seven months will be green all over. The train takes me across the expanse of Texas, across the tough roots of all the wildflowers I remember. Year after year they come back, gay and sprightly, no matter how hard the freeze in winter or how bad the August burn.

After that trip I have been remembering, my life turned over.

Miss V put me in charge of the high school station; she was a pro and, some thought, a slave driver and although she favored me, or because she did, she was on me especially hard. Every day she would ask how the new script on which I was working was coming. "Oh," I would tell her, "it is."

"Like it was yesterday? When it was also coming? Do you want to be in charge?"

"I want to be in charge, Miss V." I wanted to be like her, victorious.

"Then learn how to meet a deadline and how to write a script that will play."

My radio play, A Basket of Flowers, was subtitled, A Drama of Spring. When I sent it off it had never been performed and only Marion Van De Meyer and Julia Winter had seen the script.

I had written about three little girls, best friends until two of them begin to grow up faster than the other, and begin to wish to separate themselves from her, and from all childhood rituals and games.

The play opens on May Day in the school hall where the friends, after biking to school, are scheduled to meet, the metal baskets of their bicycles filled with small straw ones which hold spring flowers.

The narrator says that for the last several years the children have on the first of May met in the school hall in just this way and together delivered throughout the surrounding neighborhood many baskets of flowers.

The youngest girl has been standing in the hall waiting for her friends for sometime, waiting and looking out at the sky which is black with rain clouds and threatening. "I wonder when they are going to come," she says. "I hope it won't be raining."

Then we hear the giggling voices of her friends, named, the narrator tells us, April and June after those spring and summer months. After some preliminary conversation that establishes their ages, nearly thirteen, they tell their friend, little March who is still only eleven, that they are going to spend the day at the town's new teen club where this very morning a juke box is being installed. "Come with us," June says, though her tone is not really inviting. After a pause during which the listener hears only the wind blowing, the younger girl says she means to deliver the flowers.

Her friends tell her she's still a baby, that delivering flowers is boring and, they have realized, dumb, a dumb thing for little kids to do. Then they run off and we hear their scuffling steps, yelling back at her, "Oh, March, you're such a baby."

I long ago lost this script, but I remember the drama ending with March calling, "April! June! Come back."

And them retorting, "No, we don't like you anymore."

And then March crying, "Oh, the weather's so stormy." And the narrator telling the listening audience that for March it was a ruined spring.

I remember the wind machine going "Whooo, whooo, whoo" and the sound man throwing a Benny Goodman record on.

Then more giggling and shuffling and the wind machine again. And then the narrator saying the youngest child's flowers had been blown out of their baskets and into the school yard, were scattered in the dirt there and in the school building where some had also drifted across the cold stone floor.

Well, it was all a little heavy and too obviously symbolic. But in my adolescence I justified that by telling myself and others that life was.

Hadn't my two best friends from the grade school in the refinery town deserted me in just that way? Friends I had met before I met C.C. and now she was way ahead of me and going.

And hadn't other people's friends, in ways similar to the ones I dramatized, deserted them, too?

Didn't nature, time itself, separate people who loved one another?

I had wanted to tell about that, like the preacher in C.C.'s church wanted to "sing out the story."

More than that, in what I saw even then as a vain attempt, I wanted to make a metaphor for emotion and its passing. Wanted to name it, explain it, tell others. Especially the beloved.

You see, here we have it. This is what it was or is.

Joe, if I could only write to you.

West Texas

I would say: A Flower of the Field. That's what it was, all that feeling that sprang up between us.

That's what I've wanted to tell you, Joe, and looking out at all this dirt and sand reminded me. Six months ago fields to the east were covered with bluebonnets as they were thirty some years ago when I went to Dallas because I had won a contest with a five page script. Even then you were just in Texas for a visit.

You had stayed on in Europe where you had done so much broadcasting during the war. Were with us only for the spring, my charmed one, from France. The night after the broadcast, two hours of shows written and produced by high school and junior college students, you walked me out of the back of the big frame house which contained, more or less, the party for winners. The house, as I remember, was out of town, up toward Denton, off a red country road.

We faced a field alive with wildflowers and you stopped in mid-sentence and never got back to what you were going to tell me about writing radio plays.

"Those," you said, pointing. "I've missed them. They come back every year. I love those little flowers."

I still remember, as you spoke, your dark face and big, dark eyes shining and your hair, with only one little streak of white in it. I also remember thinking when I saw you years after, that it was odd, that solitary white streak, and even odder that you never got another.

"I love those little flowers."

Just last March you wrote me about them, after the train ride you had taken from Dallas to Austin and what I think of as rich-black-dirt country, though, mostly, its rolling and green. At the end of the paragraph, the first of your letter, you said, as you had back then, "I love Texas."

Well, you didn't live in it much.

Remember how you said, when we first met, "Don't tell me you are Leona Bell's daughter: She opened KTHS up in Arkansas where I put on an early radio play. When I first began I worked all the Southwestern states."

"Yes," I said, "Leona Bell is my mother."

"Well, then, Elizabeth," you were in those days always so formal with your 'Elizabeths,' "there's no help for you." You opened your arms as if to release the station to me. "All this is in your blood."

Later you told me I had learned my grit from my mother. Hardly news to me. "No woman has more grit than a Texas woman." That was what you said. I admired no one more than my mother. But her trouble terrified me. And sometimes I railed against her so I could break away.

On my last trip here I saw Dan Rodriguez in downtown Dallas. He was a programmer for KSD and had several announcing spots. Like me he has been pretty faithful to radio, has never done television much. He has opted for commercial radio and he makes good money at it, though not the kind I once thought he would go for. He took me out to lunch and we talked about those early days we worked together when I first met you, and afterward we browsed through Cokesbury bookstore where we ran into another high school friend, one I never spoke to you much about, a girl named Gerry. She has her own ad agency now and carries several important accounts. She and her mother were so poor back in Corpus, lived way out in the country in a dark, nearly windowless, frame house. Like me she hadn't any father. "My word," Gerry said, "I always did say to C.C. that you and Dan would finally wind up together."

"Oh it's only business, Gerry," I told her. And, of course, it was.

"Why are you going with that radio boy?" my Aunt Rena used to ask me and I didn't say, couldn't have then, "Aunt Rena, I'm in love with radio."

Dan wouldn't have wanted me or anybody in love with him. Even at sixteen he was too ambitious to lose work time.

From our high school class I think Dan and I are the only two people who have stayed single. Even Gerry had a try at marriage. In the early sixties I lost track of Ben. He married one of his young history teachers, then became a history teacher, a full professor at the University of Chicago now. Even in high school I knew he wasn't cut out to be a lawyer.

I never told you about Ben did I Joe? Or about any of these people. There's a whole lot I never told you. And I wanted to.

One day yet I may sit down and tell you all of our stories. Not that there's any sense of urgency.

When I first met you I felt you already knew.

Knew about Bo, and before him, Leeland. And Grandaddy and Aunt Rena. And understood about my mother whom you, you alone, just plain loved.

It was as if they were your kinfolk, too.

Later
near Austin

You had told me about your family, how your mother's people were poor and struggling and some of them shiftless, but also about how they were a people of sense and more or less of stability. Oh yes, you had told me all about your mother's striving family and about your father's half crazed one, ambitious and gifted but tormented, drunken uncles and, more hushed, drunken aunts, and men and women who couldn't get jobs. All of them, like mine, had been woodsmen, builders, teachers. And one or two had inclinations toward art.

Oh, our families were just the same. "Our families," you told me once, "built Texas."

"One of these days Leona's going to burn up," I once heard Grandma say when she heard my mother yelling at Bud.

And I can still hear Aunt Rena saying, "Well, I'm not sure what's the matter with Leona."

"I know what's the matter," I would tell her. "She didn't get to finish what she started trying for. And stopping like that broke her heart."

Joe, you always said she was the kind to do things. It hurt her, Joe, to stop doing, and even more to have the man she stopped doing for drive right off the Texas coast. And when he was gone and she was alone for a long time it was hard supporting me.

Oh Grandma always said, "Leona was this wild dark-haired thing. I couldn't keep her in the house. She was always outside in the woods and in the fields with the men, and she rode Bob, that high-spirited horse, bareback right over the side of the mountain without asking permission and that was a scandal; we would have to take the razor strap to her. She wasn't even twelve years old."

"That was one trouble," Rena said, "they all tried to break her. When she was sixteen you know she had a kind of breakdown and before she went off herself to work and study music for awhile they had to take her out of school." And then Rena would laugh! "Oh, but, she was the only one who could break Bob and, honey, he was the craziest horse I've ever seen."

"They used to whip him," my mother said. "I never had to." She started the same way every time she told me. "One day when I saw Lloyd whipping him I said, 'You had better stop that. If you don't, one day I'm going to use that thing on you.' He stopped then because he knew I meant business."

And, Joe, she did, too. Everybody in the family stopped whipping and riding Bob soon after.

Corpus, why am I writing to Joe? He's gone. The past is gone, the world sinking and Texas in it. But why go on like this? You are there. And I'm not, and am never going to be, crazy. These letters are all, of course, to you.

Corpus, Joe thought my mother was a queen. "I'll tell you, Elizabeth," he always said to me, "she has got it. She's something royal. When I was just a teenager and told him, on that weekend I went to Dallas, a few of my troubles, he said I shouldn't fuss with my mother so much about wanting to go far away to study, that she would come around. "Why," he would say, "when she was your age she scrapped for what she wanted." Yes, I thought, but she also broke down, keeps having little breakdowns. But I knew he was right, of course.

Later when she met him, my mother really liked Joe; there weren't too many men with whom she hit it off.

"The Grand Old Guy," that's what Dan always called him; he would have hated that, the name, partially, my fault since I told Dan how Joe had been on hand for the opening of the radio stations in two neighboring states. Three if we counted New Mexico.

"Why the fuck wouldn't I count New Mexico?" Dan asked. He never talked that way when we were back in high school, but like the rest of us, tried to keep up to date.

"Well," I said and this was years ago, back in the sixties, "Why would anybody? It might as well be on the moon." In my mind the world stopped with Big Bend, coyotes and rattlers and stinging scorpions under the creosote bushes and Spanish dagger. All of that near Valentine, a town we passed not too long ago on the train.

It was through Dan that I met Joe. Met Joe for the second time I mean. I was past my middle forties. Before I went to the Midwest and National Public Radio I had worked for Dan at KSD in Dallas and, before that, in Ft. Worth. Dan had scheduled Joe for an interview at the Dallas station and I had never seen him, Dan, more nervous.

I was nervous too. I dreaded explaining that we had met when I was just a kid. I didn't think he would remember. But he did, dimly, and we just got on from the first. I can still remember telling Dan, "He's so nice."

Also, and this is what I didn't say to Dan, beautiful. Tall and thin, sinewy with nice shoulders, remarkable I thought then for a man in his sixties, his arms still shapely, his hair barely streaked with white. My own which, as you know, has had ashy spots since childhood is now half grey and I've given up trying to cover it all with color. Only once before, when I met Joe as a kid, had I come face to face with such vitality; it bubbled over. He had such plans for the station! He was there, you see, to help with programming and to do a few shows.

Joe was the first person I had met in radio, at least since Marion Van De Meyer, our beloved Miss V, who made me feel I ought to work harder. I hadn't been around him ten minutes before I began to have some clear ideas on ways I might improve.

I told Joe I had met Floyd Tillman's wife once on the train, I was always a great train rider, and believed if I called her, I might get Floyd to the station to be interviewed and to play and sing a few songs. Floyd, as you may remember, was the father of country music. I added that Frances had told me that in the early days Floyd, along with Hank Williams and Eddie Arnold, worked in radio a lot.

"He worked for both KTHS and KPRC," Joe said. "And he was fired from both for plugging his songs. Afterwards I think he may have gone to KLPR in Oklahoma City. But he is a real musician, never gave a damn about fame or money. Would have lived in a tent if he could have played and composed."

I told Joe I thought Frances was a singer but quit because she wanted all the limelight to be on Floyd. She said she had seen too many marriages go bust over double ambition. Right then I made a mental note never to marry. "Not that Floyd was really ambitious," she told me. "He is too much of an artist for that. But I just want him safe."

Not long after we talked about the Tillmans, Joe disappeared to call Kate. "What's she like?" I asked him our first evening together at dinner and he said, "She's a singer."

I waited for more and he saw that. Of course I knew she was a singer, from Michigan, when Joe met her a Yank abroad; just his age or a year or two older or younger, she had been part of his first broadcasts for the BBC after the war. She had kept her voice, still did concerts.

He repeated, "She's a singer." He thought he had said it all, but to please me, he winked and added, "Elizabeth, Kate's show biz." Then he made a little gesture with his right hand. "Getting it all on. Getting on the eyeshadow, getting on the mascara." Winked again then in a theatrical way and tugged at his shiny tie. "It's everything to her," he told me, then cleared his throat and said, "Kate is strong."

I didn't know how to put all this together. Wasn't he important to her? I thought he surely was, yet there was something pejorative in that "It's everything" and in that "Kate is strong." Remembering an old country western song with the title "Prison Bars Are Strong," I almost asked, "Like prison bars are strong?"

But I didn't dare ask anything. I only told Joe that I couldn't really get a picture of Kate. I had, of course, read about her, who hadn't? For years the Texas papers were full of Joe Copeland in England and of his Midwestern wife, and he ended the discussion by saying, "She's a voice."

That made me want to hear her, made me want to go out and dial her on the phone, but, of course, it wasn't a sensible idea and anyway, I couldn't.

I had to call Frances Tillman.

When I did she was just as friendly as I remembered and sweet with lots of spice; when I told her that, she made barbs about the name of the town that she and Floyd lived in, Spicewood. Of course she would talk to Floyd she said. He was out playing golf but when he came in she would have him call me. She thought he would be glad to do it.

And he was.

On the night of the broadcast Floyd wore an open throated striped shirt, Joe a white one with the usual elegant Italian silk tie. Joe was such a mix of homey and worldly, elegant and plain. Both Floyd and Joe were in a mellow mood and when Floyd sang some of his standards, "I Love You So Much It Hurts," "I Gotta Have My Baby Back" and the song he was most famous for, country western's first cheating song, "Slipping Around," I thought I had never heard him in more plaintive voice. Afterwards he talked about his beginnings in the 1930s and also about hard times as Joe in his warm and inimitably intimate voice continued the interview. Who wouldn't tell Joe anything I wondered.

After it was all over, two weeks of broadcasting, one of them devoted to Van Cliburn whom I also met, and all of this for rebroadcast on the BBC, Joe and I said our reluctant good-byes. For days after I felt as if I were floating.

Then he was doing a job for the BBC, taping material in a number of cities; he called me from Paris, he called me from Cairo.

Toward the end of our conversations he always said, "Send word to me here. I love to hear from you. Write or call." As if I had the money for trans-Atlantic dialing, or even always knew where he was.

When I did know, I wrote him letters which sometimes he was slow to answer, but then he would and with lines that read, "Forgive my slow answers. Send more news. I'm here."

He told me once he carried my letters with him everywhere, put them all around him on the floor of his hotel rooms, that they fanned out from him like rays of light or spokes of a wheel.

"It's all right about your slow answers," I wrote, "for I know you are there. I'm very patient really." He quickly said that delighted him and that he felt on top of the world. "Oh, the world is large with so much in it!"

After that I didn't hear for months.

Then I had a postcard with spring flowers on it. "I'm glad you're patient," it said. "Happy Valentine." He had drawn a heart for February 14, the day he wrote. He must not have mailed the card until weeks later; it came to me in March.

I wrote him that his message made me happy. I didn't hear for a while after that.

After we began it was hard to say which of us was the most impulsive, which the most reticent.

But always we did more talking than writing as if as radio people we had to depend on voice. We talked about the shows we were doing and our schedules and also, oddly, with some real interest and seriousness about the weather. The Southwesterner in both of us maybe. Odd that Joe and I had early chosen to spend so much of our lives cooped up in radio stations, so often windowless and dark, because both of us were happiest out of doors.

We also talked about our birthdays which fell close together. Should I be depressed I asked now that I had passed my middle forties? He laughed. "Should I be depressed to have passed my middle sixties? Oh baby—" That was the first time he called me baby. "Oh baby, you are going into something gorgeous."

Well, it was another spring before I really was, March and spring in Texas. Months past our actual birthdays. But back in the fall we had promised each other that when we were next together we would split a cake.

The one we got, a plain white and the choice of both of us, was the best I ever ate.

"Darling," he said to me that afternoon, we had stopped at Safeway for the candles we had forgotten and picked up a number of packs, "I'm so happy to be here. So happy we are going to do this in all this open country."

Joe used endearments as if he had invented them and had never said them to anyone before but me, peppered his speech with "sweethearts" and "darlings" all that afternoon.

And I, I, each time astonished, Joe had always been so formal, as if for the first time in my life I had been given hearing, I asked, "Joe, is happiness important?"

He took some time to answer, but before he brought the car there by the side of the field to a gentle halt, and he was the slowest, the most careful of drivers, he took my hand and pressed it and uttered a resounding, "Yes."

"Jesus," Dan said to me when Joe was hospitalized for the first time, "emphysema, that's terrible. I didn't know Joe was a smoker."

"Three packs a day. Sometimes more. Or that's what he tells me. You didn't know because he never smokes at a station. He makes it up in other places; it's been impossible for him to give it up, but I think he is going to try now." Then I told Dan that of course Joe was going to get better.

Believe it or not, one of Grandma's old oilcloths was with us, a particularly durable red that throughout my life I had kept in the trunk of my cars and transferred to Joe's rented Buick and when we stopped I threw it on the ground first thing. "Sweetheart," Joe said, "this is certainly the spot."

For a while, before he came back, I tried ignoring his notes, his phone calls, tried to be suitably in the mood for renunciation. His marriage was a rock for him; I was even half-glad he had it. We had to keep clear, had to keep straight. I tried putting him out of my mind.

Silly as this sounds I went out and bought myself all white bed covers and a white nightgown and when I crawled in my nun's bed let go, surrendered, all I had been feeling. What I thought I wanted.

What I thought he had wanted too.

How many times had he told me, "What you know, Elizabeth, what I know, is work."

And yet here we were in this field north of Dallas, the past repeating itself, the landscape so familiar that I wondered if this was the same field we came to when I was just sixteen. I watched a flock of white birds sail around the cows crouching beneath its one live oak tree.

We dropped down beside the oilcloth laughing. Before us stretched acres and acres of grass and little blue and white flowers. I tried to be gentle with the cake.

He had told me, "Oh, I want to be with you in the country, want to breathe all that good air now that I can again."

We had potato salad and breast of chicken sandwiches in the basket Joe had carried and a thermos of Brazilian coffee from a coffee house in Dallas and, mostly for me—Joe couldn't have much, he had been under oxygen in the hospital—a sweet white wine. Joe was going to have to partake of our feast slowly, but it was always good being together. We always had such a good time.

When we were ready for the cake Joe said he had to load it with candles, that our combined years came to more than a hundred. "One hundred and twelve to be exact," he told me and then insisted, laughing, coughing just a little, that we get on all of that. "Well, it's time we get it all on," he said, looking at me and winking, "not that I can blow any of it out."

We made jokes about that. I thought our humor was becoming grotesque.

"There are too many of these to go out," I said as I stuck in a bunch of candles, "hardly matters if you and I are huffing and puffing over them or not." He held my left hand, he was a firm hand holder, his smile and eyes right on me as I lit them with my right. Then, just before we tried to blow the candles out, his expression changed.

"Well," he said, "if I called you more often, if we were together more often, it would never stop, but just go on and on."

"Oh," I whispered in that conflicted moment, "wouldn't that be fine?"

But he didn't answer. Only said, "Then we would both be crazy."

The implication seemed to be that he already was. "That first day I met you I missed lunch with the network president, missed afternoon drinks with the governor."

"Joe," I asked, "what are you talking about?"

He didn't answer, only grazed my cheeks with his lips. "Baby," was all he said.

Austin

Although there was that time when I stopped writing letters, so we could just stop, when Joe wrote me to send word, I sent it.

I no longer had a job with National Public Radio or any other kind.

After which he wrote me about a number of public stations he thought could use me in the west. He had been in and out of L.A. for more than a year; he had even bought a small Laurel Canyon house. I should come out right away he said; he wanted me near and for a while, before he had to go to Australia and New Zealand for BBC broadcasts he thought he could help me get started. We talked about it on the phone.

"Joe?" I asked right after I picked up the receiver. I don't know why; we hadn't talked in a while and, besides, I was staying with a friend so he shouldn't have known how to find me. But I knew it was Joe before I heard his voice.

"You *are* there," he said. "I just got this phone number from your Mama."

"You have just talked to my mother?" I wasn't sure how; I didn't think she was in any book. I remember that I had written him once on her business stationery from Nacogdoches.

"We just taught a piano lesson together, she had a student there. I told her what a fan I had been of hers. We just hit if off."

I had been chopping vegetables all that hot morning, my mind on Aunt Rena and how she loved them, parsley and green onion up to my elbows, all over my hands and arms.

Then Joe gave me names of directors at several stations. "Now wipe your hands," he said, "and go call them." How did he know, I wondered, that my hands needed wiping?

"To live out there," I asked, "doesn't it cost a lot of money?"

"Darling," he said, "you can live on sunshine and the sight of flowers." Then he told me about oranges and avocados because I had said, "Joe, you know how I love to eat."

But it didn't take me long to decide.

After I had, he said, "You make me so happy sweetheart."

One day back at KSD in Dallas, Joe, getting ready for a broadcast in his usual flurry, shuffling papers, polishing his glasses and then the mike with a trouser tissue, looked straight at me and from out of the blue, said, "We get it all mixed up, don't we, soul and body?"

And I, in my ungrown up, uncompromising way asked, "Wasn't it meant to be?"

He flinched a little at that. And sounded angry.

"Well, hell," he said, oh, Corpus, how well you taught us to say this, "we can work together. Hell, that's finally what it's all about. Day after day putting one foot in front of the other. When you get right down to it, the thing to say is that we are both workers. I can work with you."

I was glad he said that, but a little angry, too. I knew Kate was his refuge and never mind what else he had said about their marriage, the loss of desire, the loss of the body. He had married Kate late; when he met her had all but given up the idea of marrying. As had she. But they got along. "Oh," he told me, "both of us were ready!" Married they would have a plan, construct something. In London and New York they established and maintained households, built a life.

Just a few months before, at the Dallas station, I heard Joe talking to Dan about someone Dan had been seeing and about "lust."

Are you talking to Dan about what you feel for me, Joe? I had wanted to ask. I hate that split that severs spirit from body.

Did Joe worry that what he felt would split him off like that from me? Everyone I knew seemed hurt by that severing. Body from spirit, body from mind.

Dan had been talking about a topless dancer he met at one of the clubs. Someone he had been going to bed with or maybe I should say someone he had been screwing. Dan didn't go to bed for the night with anybody. Or so he confessed to me. After he had as much of a woman as he wanted, that is, when he took the time to actually meet one and take her home, he would help her get dressed and into a taxi and in the process, put a gold or silver bracelet on one of her wrists, or, around her neck, a necklace of semi-precious stones. He told me once he spent hundreds and hundreds of dollars every year on women's jewelry.

As I walked in on Joe's conversation with Dan—it was one that took place just before a show and as many thousand shows as Joe had done, he was always nervous—as I walked in on the conversation I said, "I'm going to look that word up in the dictionary."

"What word is that, darling?"

"Lust," I said.

I slapped the script that I had just been over down on the shiny table. "It is in the dictionary, isn't it?" Not just in the Bible? I almost asked that but bit my tongue. Your fucking Methodist Bible.

Joe had been brought up in Methodist and other Protestant churches. I almost said—you read it often enough for one who is never in a church. He did read it, too, though he didn't take them literally, quoted scripture and verse.

I didn't say any of that, but might as well have, for he surmised my meaning. "Elizabeth," he said, "you're tired."

"No," I told him. "No, Joe, I'm not tired."

I picked up the dictionary then. There was one on the table at the far end of the room.

"Then what's wrong?"

"Nothing's wrong, Joe. I'm just trying to get an education, trying to discover meaning."

"You know what it finally means, honey," he interjected. "Craziness. And that won't quit. Torment, baby."

That began the first argument we had. We only had one other and it was toward the end in California and of a gentler kind.

It came just before he took off for Australia, the BBC taping there. I think even then I was angry at him for being sick and that, in spite of his hospitalizations and the difficulty we knew he often had in breathing, none of us acknowledged how serious the sickness was. I can't imagine why else I would have started anything, why under any other circumstances I would have said anything so awful.

We had been talking around something when I said, "I don't believe in the survival of personality." Said that quite suddenly.

Said that to Joe. And I knew deep down that he was dying.

He was even then beginning to lose his radio voice, the voice that was his life and dollar and that he was famous for. He looked at me fiercely, steadily and replied in a whisper, "I do."

I hated myself, hated my anger, my stupid blundering. And tried to make things better.

But made them worse.

"What I mean is, I don't believe we go on as we are here," I laughed nervously. "Radio people, brunets, Texans."

Family people, I wanted to add, flower-lovers, cake eaters.

So strange that I had said that; certainly I couldn't imagine Joe as anything but a radio person; if he was anything else, would he have meant anything to me?

"What I mean is," I went on, my voice getting weaker, I was sounding sillier and sillier even to myself, "what I mean is, I think we have to undergo some sort of drastic change. Become nothing before we do it. Nothing, or almost—"

Then Joe looked angry, too. He cleared his throat. "Well, then," he said and his voice had come back to him, "well then, I think that's going to be exciting. I would like to get on with that." For a minute I thought he might say that when he did he would do a broadcast.

"Damn it," I wanted to tell him, "it's too soon for you to want to get on with it."

We were in a parked car, another of the ones Joe had rented, as we talked like this; Joe had driven me home from the station to my tiny apartment here on 11th Street and sat straight behind the wheel.

I hated the rigid way he held his body, the way he looked absently out the window. Already he seemed far from me. I leaned toward him, touched his face, then kissed it and with one hand touched his beautiful dark hair. He gathered me to him then.

"Darling, there's nothing to do, there's no help for it." He held me close. I was sobbing and continued to sob as I clung onto him and pressed into him, my hands sliding across his shoulders, wishing as he kissed my neck, my ears, my hair, my face all over that we could both in this moment disappear. "We've waited so long to have this. We love each other," he said.

Los Angeles
January 6, Epiphany

His mouth brushed back and forth, one side to the other and again and again, across my mouth. "Breathe with me," he whispered; I parted my lips, was very still, gave him breath.

But we couldn't go on like that. We never had a weekend or even a whole night together; it was as if those waited in some far country in which we were both free and where there was no sickness. Often when Joe had to go home, or to the doctor, and I had to go back to the station we nuzzled each other in the car like two teenagers who hankered after some distant life.

He became too sick to work, to see me, often had a hard time speaking over the phone. When he did improve he packed a bag full of medicine, packed oxygen, and in spite of his doctor's warning, left for Australia. Before he left he came by the station once.

"We don't see each other anymore," I told him.

"We'll see each other when I get back. When I'm better." But he spoke without conviction.

He said, "I hope you get on here." Then said in a halting broken-hearted voice, "I love you."

He ran a hand across my back and kissed me on the mouth, lightly, but with great sweetness and quite publicly, several times.

Corpus, is your festival still held on Thursday, the first after Trinity Sunday? The Feast of Corpus Christi, Mexican children running through your streets turning their little musical wheels? I remember the ringing going on and on and now think of the celebration as something to hear, a cacophony of bells.

"We celebrate two thousand years of His living and dying," I still remember the priest saying, his Mass reaching me through my shiny white radio, a graduation present from Bud. "And we celebrate this place. Corpus Christi. This cathedral consecrated to Corpus Christi and to all our living and dying."

He went on to say that the bay was named by Alonzo Alverez de Pineda, a Jamaican explorer who mapped the Texas coast line and brought the first white men to Texas and whose ship arrived on this very day.

Mexican people do celebrate dying. With dancing and skeletons and bread for the dead and laughter. And they believe the dead visit and partake.

Yesterday in East Los Angeles where little English is spoken I went to a service with a Mariachi band and glittering Aztec dancers who, barefoot in skin tight sequined costumes and enormous feathered head dresses, carried torches as they gyrated up and down the aisles. I sang half a dozen hymns in Spanish and embraced that many people at the Paz. And afterwards ate homemade tamales and drank Margaritas by the glassful and felt for a moment as if I knew again what birth and death, our own and Jesus Cristo's, are about.

Back in you, Corpus, we were Mexican and Anglo alike taught that the spirit goes on though we must give up the body. Dark skin over shapely shoulders, amber eyes, luminous hair.

It had been hard to get my life on the line. Joe finally put me on it, then slipped away.

After his trip to Australia and in, of all places, New Zealand.

The BBC, of course called Kate immediately and not long after, all the papers publicized her grief. But no one told me, no reason why Kate should have; I only met her once. I heard about it over the radio, a rival station of the two I worked for.

Corpus, I recently traveled fifteen hundred miles across the state of Texas and never even saw you. In memory I walk thirteen steps up your seawall, visit the old Nueces again where we held some dances. And, on the bluff, past the Driscol and the Plaza, then drift to the cathedral where your festival was held.

Although I don't go often, go always feeling like a transient, and don't trust orthodoxy, I have once again taken to churches. You may remember my telling you about the one I like best here, the one that feeds the hungry, provides help for the addicted.

I'm in Hollywood to work at that church today.

Some days before Communion I think I see Uncle Leeland standing alongside my pew like an usher. At other times I see Grandaddy, as far as I knew he was never in an Episcopal church in his life, and just last Sunday in the pew in front of me I saw Miss V, her V-shaped wings, spread behind her, and Julia Winter. In that moment I knew she never had a fiance, that we made her fiance up. And at The Peace both turned to face me, smiling. Then, standing by Cecil B. DeMille's Ten Commandments, I saw Bud in the narthex. He and my mother split up just a year or two before he died and I never did know exactly what was the trouble. As I step out into the sunshine I think he may be speaking to me, but what I hear finally is another voice.

"Lady, I only have two cans of soup in the house and three little children. Can you give me something?"

"Not much," I tell her, pulling a dollar from my purse. "See the Father."

Just then a flock of Korean children run by me.

Earlier I told you the church had no children, and at that time, there were only one or two in the English speaking congregation. I am conscious of places without children since I have none.

What I haven't told you: the church has services in Korean every Sunday and a Korean-American congregation who have many children. And last week the sight of them as they passed me cheered my heart.

Later

"When I was young I never had a romance," Joe told me. "I was all absorbed in family. I was going to make things right for them, going to conquer the world." He told me he had missed love.

Finally that made him furious.

A generation apart, and a gender, we had such similar histories. Our difference? He had married. Late, but at least he had finally done it. I knew marriage was a relationship like no other, bonded, involved intimacies, like no other. He met Kate during the war and her career took off after she was in some of his overseas shows.

Also a difference: His greater calling and ambition. No dynamo, I had never really considered "conquering the world."

But I certainly did want to make things right for my family, accomplish for Uncle Leeland and Uncle Bo. And, yes, Grandma. And Lloyd and all the others I hadn't known. (Also a drinker, Lloyd died suddenly after a fall down a flight of warehouse stairs.) Call them back and extend what each of them had tried to begin. What my mother did begin. Most of all I wanted to make things right for her.

Corpus, you taught us that spirit goes on and love is lasting, though maybe not us who contain it and through which it passes. Who move, change, go.

Who knew what it was that after so many years finally broke my mother and Bud up?

When he was drunk Bo railed against Leona. And so did I that summer before I went to college, the college in a place much farther away than she thought I ought to go. Before Bud called the police and later signed the papers that committed him to the state hospital, Bo had threatened my mother with a knife. Yet she always defended Bo to Bud. And it was Bud, not Bo, who she finally dismissed from her life.

I pondered their breakup a lot.

Bud held unsteady jobs; she never fulfilled her musical promise. They both had tempers and, I realized, heavy responsibility for me and, after his breakdown, for Uncle Bo, were tied to Uncle Bo. Nor would Bo, as much as he complained about the shackles of his family, let them go. Still, none of that seems enough.

In retrospect I see they both grew up in a country that blighted erotic feeling, and several other generating kinds, that removed it from spirit and made of it a sin.

Although they were still together the summer I graduated from high school, their relationship was stormy. One was forever lashing out against the other and at least twice they had fights in which they threw things, shoes, books, keys, cups and saucers. During the last of these, after Leona had thrown a cup of coffee, Bud socked her in the face and knocked her to the kitchen floor leaving on her cheek the impression of his Masonic ring.

I didn't see him do this and I wouldn't have believed it. But the design of the ring, which forever after I thought of as "Bud's mark," was there. That she had been knocked flat by it was hard for me to comprehend. I had always thought of my mother as so strong. Bud had been nice to me, if distant. But he threatened Uncle Bo.

"Hell," I heard Bud yell across the yard to the porch, one of those first hot nights before my graduation, the thick air potent with the smell of gas and gardenias, "Hell's bells! You piss ant. Come down from there! I want it out with you. Let's you and me take a walk down to the vacant lot. I want you to fight with me like a man."

Bud had, I think, heard Bo talking about him to Grandma—this was just a few nights before she died—about how another one of Bud's jobs had ended and how Bud and my mother were back on him again, about how he would never be free of his sister or her child or her man. I believe this was the night right after my senior party. I can still smell the gardenias. To this day I associate their perfume with death, not to its sadness, but to the cleansing agent in it.

To the power that sweeps mercifully away.

Bud had for a long time been tired of being with our family and he knew it was Bo who tied him and my mother to us. If he thought Bud's job was OK, Bo was always on the phone begging, "Come back to me!" And if he knew Bud's job had played out, he was on it saying, "I have secure work; I'm here to come back to."

What Bud said must have scared Bo half to death. He ran like a rabbit from the challenge, ran into the house and through it and onto the back patio and into the yard and through the bright gate to the driveway where Bo hopped in the car. He didn't come back until all the lights were out in the house and the garage apartment, after midnight I heard the sound of the tires against the gravel drive.

For me it was such a strange summer, strange to be out of high school, my glorious career there over, to be out in the work-a-day, working-class world. For Bo it must have been even stranger. Strange to be without his mother, have his house on the market, be engaged to a girl he was afraid to marry and in love with and estranged from a beautiful young man. He had the courage for none of this nor even enough to answer my stepfather's accusations.

He decided at the last minute to drive me east to college and that he could pay for it; he really couldn't and the pressure of trying to pay so many bills contributed to his crack up. I had decided at the last minute that east was the direction in which I had to go.

Travis had left you, Corpus, and C.C. couldn't share her grief, rage or sorrow. But I didn't know that then; I thought she didn't want to see much of me. That summer I saw little of my high school friends.

Except Bartola. From July on he was around. And I felt a kinship.

One reason maybe: My job was awful.

I had always, all my life, when I went to bed at night looked forward to the morning. But I didn't anymore. And I wondered if Bartola also dreaded each day.

He was a mystery to me, but there was something in him, something reckless and wild, some loveliness, that I responded to. That plus the torment that I could tell was in him. The torment that I and all my family knew.

Although at school we had conversations, I didn't really get to know Bartola until both of us went to work. We met here and there, in front of a movie house or down by the seawall, and once or twice in his store. Bartola worked that summer selling cheap costume jewelry, bracelets and earrings and rings, as a clerk at Kress's. Every time I saw him at Kress's he tried to convince me to buy a birthstone ring.

"But my birthstone's a garnet," I told him. "They don't cost much. If I save I can get a real one someday; in fact, I plan to."

He didn't seem to know what to say.

"You going to college, Elizabeth?" he asked me. His voice, hoarse and high at once and the same time, was barely a whisper, his eyes, framed by the thick, long lashes, almost closed.

"Yes," I told him. "I guess so."

I told him I didn't know exactly what I wanted to do, that I had been lost since graduation. I said I hated my job at Litchenstein's where I worked in accounting, typing numbers all day. I said that as soon as I got off at night I started dreading the morning.

Bartola opened his eyes wide then and shrugged his silky, hot pink shoulders. "Well, honey, look at me. I even have to work Saturdays." He sighed and picked through the rings, held up a gold one with an insert of lavender glass. "You like this? Isn't it pretty? I'll bet it would almost fit you."

I shook my head.

"Aw, come on, Elizabeth, some of this stuff isn't so bad. Maybe one of the green ones. Baby, real emeralds are expensive. What time do you get your lunch? How do you like this for $2.95?" He held up a large chunk of electric green.

He knew I wasn't going to buy it. I told him I had to go, but before I did we agreed to meet early in the week at the seawall and eat sack lunches there while looking at the lucky people who had their freedom and could sail boats in the bay. We surely couldn't linger; neither of us had a full hour for lunch.

The next Tuesday was, as things turned out, one of overpowering brightness. I wore a black sundress which I thought of as defense. A white one would have been cooler.

Bartola winked when he saw me, slowly closing one of his gorgeous golden eyes. If I had gone looking for his black eyelashes at Kress's or even at Litchenstein's, I couldn't have found them. "You look so sophisticated, Elizabeth. You ought to travel. You ought to use your college money to go to the south of France or to Spain.

I told Bartola there wasn't any college money, only the Installment Plan and Bo's labor. None of my teachers talked scholarship, or even loan, to me. They thought Bo had money. Scholarships were for kids who lived in a couple of rented rooms with a single parent or for those with many brothers and sisters. Not that any of us needed a bundle. Most of us applied only to inexpensive state schools.

"Probably just as well," I said, "considering the trouble I have with language." After three years of high school French, neither Bartola or I had learned much. More disturbing to me: I knew almost no Spanish, the language that three-quarters of our population read and spoke. And during the Christmas and Easter seasons we had hundreds of additional Mexican visitors who came to you, Corpus, because of your name.

But when I told Bartola that he said I shouldn't worry, that no one in Corpus did much better. "They speak Tex-Mex here," he told me, "not Spanish." He claimed his Spanish was better than most since his grandfather was from Mexico City. I doubted that his grandfather was, but, if he liked it, wanted Bartola to keep this fantasy.

And, anyway, I thought, who was I to say?

Certainly Bartola's mother, a small town and yet worldly looking woman, might have grown up anywhere. Voluptuous but slender, Mrs. Perra was sexy. No wonder, I thought, when I talked to Bartola, that sex was the uppermost subject on his mind. "She's been attached to a few men," he told me, "but they have never given her money and she has to live in these low down clubs." She waited tables and, sometimes, was a singer. Bartola said his father left too long ago to be remembered. But, he insisted that Perra was a legal name, that his father was an Italian-born-

Italian and that his father and mother had been married in the cathedral on the bluff.

Anybody who had five minutes acquaintance with either Bartola or his mother would know how easily either of them might have made this story up. Or how easily it might be true.

"Do you believe in love?" Bartola asked as we sat on the top step of the seawall that first afternoon we were together. On the way there we passed the blind man I had seen walking the waterfront all winter, a big sign around his neck that read "Alms for the Blind." Ever since I have thought of the seawall as "Blind Man's Bluff."

"Do you believe in love?" He asked me that question before he took the warm cheese sandwiches, grilled at the Kress's counter, out of his brown paper sack. He had insisted on bringing both our lunches. "Kress's cheese sandwiches aren't bad," he told me. "They use pimento-cheese."

In addition to the sandwiches, Bartola also brought lemon cokes from the Kress's fountain, two small bags of popcorn and Hershey Bars with almonds. We gave most of our popcorn to the gulls "I mean love like in the movies," Bartola said, "a picture with Clark Gable or Tyrone Power."

I said, and I didn't know what to say, I didn't think I had seen any love like what he talked about. But as I spoke, an image of Ben flashed through my mind as well as one of Travis and C.C. In my mind Ben was behind the wheel of the car we sat in on Padre Island. I said my mother had told me once that she had been in love with my father, but I thought she might have imagined that after he went away. And that I didn't think she had been in love like this with Bud. I said I thought Aunt Rena might have been with Uncle Leeland. But then I remembered the women Uncle Leeland saw at the Elks Club. I said I thought Aunt Rena and Uncle Leeland were confused about it. "I think we are all confused about it." That's what I finally said.

"Baby," Bartola told me, "I believe in love. I'm going to have it. Going to get away from this town and maybe work in the movies. Going to California. Going to the coast."

He jangled a bunch of bracelets, pulled out of his hip pocket every color in the rainbow, then slid one over my arm. "You like one of these?" he asked.

I wrinkled my nose. "I don't wear bracelets," I told him.

These are special for a dollar fifty-nine. If you don't want them, I'll take them."

He shook the bracelets in his hand, then slipped them over one of his bare brown arms. He said, "Right here in Corpus I play parts already."

"Bartola," I told him, "you don't belong here. You ought to go to California soon. You ought to get away."

105

"Baby, I am," he told me.

And later on that noon he said, jangling the bracelets, "I'm going to have love. Going to have money. And when I have those I'll also be able to buy some really nice things."

"Oh, I'm sure you will, Bartola," I told him.

Again he jangled the bracelets. "I'm going to have LOVE," he sang as he began to dance around. Then he stopped and said quite solemnly, and softly, "You're going to have love."

"I don't think about love, Bartola," I lied, whispering. Then raising my voice I said, "And I don't care about money which is funny because I have to make some. I just want to be myself. And to work in radio. How I miss the station!" As I spoke I hated Dan Gonzales, and I had always liked Dan, whom I hadn't seen since he took the KRIS job. Next year I told myself I would apply, instead, at KEYS.

A family of gulls landed at our feet then, the bay before us still as a lake and sparkling, in spite of the heat, not blue, but brown. I gave them several handfuls of popcorn and the last of my sandwich. "Oh, Bartola," I said, "do you suppose we'll be disillusioned?"

He didn't answer and then I realized he had no idea what "disillusioned" meant. I didn't want to embarrass him. The last thing in the world he needed was more shame. "I mean," I said, "do you suppose we'll be disappointed? So disappointed that we become bitter or crooked or mean? I mean when things don't turn out?"

"Baby, everything is going to turn out," he said.

The gulls were by this time ready for the rest of my popcorn, but I didn't want to give it up. I looked beyond them to the water. "Come on, let's wade," I said to Bartola, taking his hand.

And then we were down the steps, free of shoes and even of our popcorn bags which we had dumped on the way. Bartola rolled up his sailor pants and hand in hand, we entered the hot, sticky bay. I loved the feel of it, always had, even tolerated a nip from a jelly fish or two. I was not one of those people who when they came out made a B-line for some shower. "Oh, Bartola," I asked, "won't you miss the bay?"

"After I have seen the Pacific?" He raised one of those Tyrone Power brows. It was the one feature they had in common. "Oh, Baby, no."

"They say it's a gorgeous ocean," I told him. "My Uncle Bo's friend, Jay, always says it's gorgeous, but wild, too, he says, and cold."

"If it gets too wild or cold for me," Bartola said swinging one of my hands, "I'll just hop a plane back down here. I'll have so much money that will be easy; I can come back to this bay any time I like."

On our way back we picked up our popcorn sacks from the steps and tossed them in the waste container just across the street from the seawall on the corner with the stop light, when an orange Thunderbird swerved around it and almost up onto the sidewalk where we were. The boy who was driving, and for just a second I thought I knew him, thought he was Lana's or somebody else's brother, yelled, "Hey faggot!" And then, "Hey, fag hag!"

Bartola didn't even startle. "Corpus has so many crude people," he told me. "That's why I am going to leave it. They think they're so hot. They think they have all the answers. And they're just crude and dull." Then after a pause, he added, "All the same, if they could, they would run over you."

"Bartola," I asked, and I was shy with this question, "what's a fag-hag?"

He dropped his lashes and his brown face reddened. "Someone who hangs around people like me. A woman who does that." I had never before seen him blush. "A woman who hangs around queers."

I was quiet for awhile. Then I said, "You're my friend, Bartola. I like you for being proud of who you are. A lot of people here don't know who they are and don't want to find out."

"If they did," he said, "they wouldn't be able to stand it. But they wouldn't admit to nothing."

"Well, why think about them?" I asked.

"They're brutal, baby. You have to think about them when they nearly run over you in a fancy car."

He had to watch out for them he told me, then added that I had better watch out, too. "But I think you do watch out, Elizabeth," he went on, "though maybe you don't know that you do. That's why you won't think about love. You might find out it belonged to one of them."

I knew then why I was with him. Never mind that he didn't understand the word "disillusion"; he understood something more and in a way no one else had, not Uncle Bo or Aunt Rena or my mother or even Julia Winter, something that until that moment, and even then I only got a glimmering, I didn't understand myself.

Hollywood

C.C. married during my second year of college. The shock of her announcement was so great that nothing since has much surprised me. She had a baby in the first year and another in the second and two more before many more years had passed. She sent me all their pictures, all girls with smooth brown hair like hers, and two had her sky blue eyes, and sweet, smiling faces. And she wrote letters which, while detailing some of the struggles, made child bearing and rearing sound like the most natural process in the world.

And for her I think it was.

My placid, smooth-haired, home-based friend, my opposite in many ways and yet also an alter-ego, was gentle with herself and with her children. And had married a gentle man, a hill country lawyer, from a ranching family, who finally didn't like to practice, who took to breeding dogs, herding dogs mostly, simply because he liked them; bought and ran a kennel. And who, after a few years in Corpus where he tried to live for awhile because T.J. couldn't stand to lose her, moved back to that rolling green flowery country in the center of the state.

C.C.'s story always seemed to me to have a genuinely "happily ever after" ending for her youth, and I sometimes imagined mine. An ending which she came to quickly, even abruptly, and one I often wanted to claim.

Unlike so many fictional heroines she never seemed betrayed. But I know there is much I don't see because I view all this obliquely and at such a distance. C.C. was the first to admit that none of her children had been planned for, that they had all been born before she had a chance to comprehend what had happened to her and that she didn't know how to deal with it when she did. She wrote me once that she had been nearly overwhelmed when they were all pre-schoolers and again when they were in middle childhood, and that for a time she had seen a counselor.

And I do remember that the news of Travis's death shook her. She had been married for some years when she wrote me about him, explaining that although he learned draftsmanship in the service, he seldom used it, that he had practically become a professional soldier, had fought in several wars. She wasn't clear about which war took him, but I believe it was Vietnam. He had died of some tropical fever. Only a few days before they shipped him in a box back to you, Corpus, the State Department let his father know.

The Assembly of God members from that little church near where he had lived held a memorial service. C.C. read about it in the papers. She supposed his wife was there, his wife had come back to you, Corpus, or so C.C. said, as soon as Travis flew for the final time overseas; they didn't have any children. The Caller Times said burial was in the graveyard next to the church. C.C. speculated that Travis's father had probably done the lettering on the stone.

"It already seems so long ago," C.C. told me in her letter. "I was another person." She documented what had happened as if she was relating to the plot of a film.

After she married I kept in touch with C.C. only by card and occasional letter and, as time went on, more and more infrequently. Seven or eight years passed before we had a visit. That was my last to you, Corpus.

I have always been baffled by children, never known what to do or say around kids, anybody's, and I surely didn't around hers. I could see that the job of caring for them and of running the little house they all lived in was a hard one, but at least at the time I visited, C.C. seemed to take it in stride. Her secret, I thought, was that she always did a lot of what she liked and wouldn't take on anything she really hated. She had never learned to sew and wouldn't and she and Will hadn't been married long when she refused to give dinner parties for people who were less than friends.

Part of what she liked to do was read, to herself and also aloud to the children. When I visited she asked me to read to them, too. "Oh, please, Elizabeth," she said when I protested. "They know you're on the radio. Oh, they've heard so much about you." And so I did, although I felt awkward. Lined up in a row, little to big against the bedroom wall in their rose, green and blue flowered nightgowns, they made a picture. How silly I felt when I dropped down on the floor beside them. And so I read them something silly. ("They went to sea in a sieve," I read. "In a sieve they went to sea.") after telling them very short stories that I had made up about your keys, Corpus, Port Aransas and Mustang Islands.

C.C. had taken to framing art prints from the Impressionist and Post Impressionist period, and when my reading was through and the children were in bed, she showed me her collection. She would always love best, she said, works from the late nineteenth century. Although she still drew, and would eventually finish her degree in art and maybe even someday teach it, her own drawing didn't satisfy her and she didn't know that it ever would. More than anything else, working with these prints transported her at times when she needed transporting. "When it comes to art, I guess I am mostly a receiver," she told me. The central hall of her ranch house was lined with Renoirs and Cassatts and near the end, by the door, with Gaugins, the painter who she said best expressed her hidden yearnings. When she spoke of what she felt for these last pictures I realized she was also speaking of what she had once felt for Travis, and still felt for me.

Later

Two years went by before I saw Bartola again by the seawall, although during that first summer we were together I continued to visit him at the Kress's counter over grilled cheese sandwiches and lemon Cokes.

Winters and springs and another summer sped by quickly. And during that second summer that I was back in you, Corpus, I spied Bartola when on a late lunch hour I was walking the seawall by myself. The old blind man walked it too and later in the afternoon we put quarters in his cup.

My job that July was with the Nueces and although I still didn't like typing for a living, I tolerated my place of employment a little better because at least it was with an old hotel.

Dan still had the only summer job at KRIS, but he never contacted me and I couldn't get a job at KEYS. In the wintertime Dan worked on a degree in communications at UT. I hadn't seen Ben since I graduated, but had received some letters, which, of course I answered. Pre-law, he had gone to Northwestern on a scholarship, was working on a history degree.

The news of C.C.'s engagement during the previous winter had depressed me. It came when we were off to college just half a year when I was far away in the east and the wide world just opening to me.

I reasoned we could still be friends if she was marrying Travis. Travis was familiar or at least I had certainly heard enough of his banter at the drive-ins and on the bluff overlooking the shrimp boats and had seen his tow head bobbing up and down often enough in the front seat of the car.

But C.C. was not marrying Travis; she was marrying a stranger who lived in far away Kerrville. Had, in fact, already married him and moved there. (Although, as things turned out, she didn't stay, but came back for awhile to you, Corpus.) And not a boy either, but a man.

For me New York was exciting, but also difficult and often, a puzzle. I was beginning not to know what to think about life.

So it was that on that hot summer day when I was walking the seawall the sight of Bartola cheered me. No mistake about it; it was Bartola in his silky magenta shirt and white sailor pants.

"What are you doing here?" I asked, hugging him. I had run straight into his arms. "Are you working?" I asked. I had imagined him so many times out west.

"Oh, Baby," he told me, "would you believe it? I'm still at Kress's."

"No, I don't believe it," I said, but the moment after I was sorry. He looked so ashamed.

"The only reason I stayed," he told me, "is because I was promoted. I manage a whole section now, cosmetics and jewelry and what we have now is better. We even sell, behind the counter, some semi-precious stones. Anyway, I'm saving my money."

"But I'm so glad you're here now," I told him. "I'm so glad to see you."

"Oh, Baby, I'm glad to see you. When did you get in?"

"Weeks ago," I said. "I have a typing job at the Nueces."

"And you haven't come to see me? I'm hurt."

I told him I hadn't known he was in town. He said now that he had seen me he wouldn't take no for an answer, I was spending the evening with him.

And I did. At North Beach Bartola bought me all the corn on the cob I could eat, more than a half dozen ears as I remember, and took me on several Ferris wheel rides. And on the Ferris wheel, on the last go round, we agreed to meet for lunch at the seawall the very next day. Bartola said he would bring the lunches.

"I won't have to worry about being fired if I'm away for awhile this time," he told me. "Now they give me a whole hour." He looked so proud when he said that. Kress's had given him just twenty-five minutes before. Then he asked me, and he seemed embarrassed to be so late with the question, "They give you an hour, don't they?"

"Yes," I said.

He said, "We'll have lots of time. I'll take care of the food, don't you worry. This summer Kress's has a good turkey sandwich special. I'll bring something else, too, something extra." He winked. "A surprise."

In spite of the heat which would, of course, have melted it, I think I imagined some gooey ice cream extravaganza.

But the next day after we had eaten our sandwiches and drained our tall paper glasses of Coke and iced tea, after we had fed the birds our crusts and half our popcorn, nothing else from Bartola's sack seemed forthcoming. I thought maybe he had brought homemade pralines or some especially beautiful Mexican cookies, iced maybe in yellow or pink.

"Bartola," I asked finally, "where's my surprise? It's time you told me."

He looked pleased. He said, "You remembered."

"Well," I said, "of course. I never forget a surprise. Do you?"

"I've been saving it," he said. He smiled broadly. "Give me your hand."

"No, no," he told me moments later when I extended my left hand. "I can't marry you. Now give me your other hand."

As I held out my right hand, palm skyward, I thought he would pull some sort of delectable candy from his pocket, or a party whistle maybe, or silken streamers in purple and gold, CCHS colors. Or sparklers maybe. We both loved those.

He slipped it on then; I still have it and from time to time remove it from my jewelry box and squeeze it on a finger.

"Open your eyes now," Bartola commanded.

What I saw took my breath, a big square cut garnet set in gold filigree. "This is the new line we carry," Bartola told me. "It's real."

I wanted to tell him that I had never met anyone like him and that I loved him, as, if only in this moment, I did. But I couldn't.

No one before had ever given me a ring.

Part Three

Los Angeles

And no one since.

Bartola's ring my one and only. The garnet, I'm told is associated with all that is Victorian, antique.

"I've missed love," I told Aunt Rena. She's gone finally. I just got word about it.

"Well," she said the first day I saw her after more than twenty years of being away. We sat in lawn chairs in front of her tiny house in Shreveport, a house that was nearly on the street; she lived alone but her nephews looked after her. "Well, you never did marry and I guess you won't now. Some people marry for the first time when they are past forty, but not many. Not many marry then for the first time."

"It's too bad, " I said, "but I wasn't grown up enough for it when I grew up." I laughed. "I mean when I was through school and was, maybe twenty. I grew up, did that finally, just a year or two ago."

Joe always told me that in the region we came from people didn't grow up. Or at least not, if they did at all, until late in life. He grew up he said only after he had lived for years in Europe as a broadcaster; he met Kate during a broadcast, years after the end of World War II.

Aunt Rena looked at me the way one looks at a stranger. And I couldn't blame her. But in my whole life I had only seen her look at anyone like that but once or twice.

"Tell me about it," she said. "Tell me what happened, honey. I never thought you would stay single like all those others in your family. I guess even your Mama finally wound up single."

"I think, Aunt Rena," I told her, "I wound up even more single than any of them."

She smiled, her eyes still like Santa's, still bearers of gifts. She said, "You know when you were a girl I thought you were crazy about that little Jewish boy who came to Corpus Christi." She made him sound like the only Jewish boy who ever had. "What ever happened to him?"

I told her Ben had become a college teacher, a professor, and had married someone who was also a teacher and had children, a boy and a girl, who became teachers, or I thought one of them had become a teacher and the other maybe was a lawyer, I forget, and who, like everyone else I knew, or almost everybody, either got a divorce or talked of getting a divorce, what everyone does at forty. I said I had lost track but that we had exchanged Christmas cards for years.

"That doesn't sound natural, " she told me.

I had always considered Aunt Rena an authority on what was natural in life.

Which leads me back in memory to the mystery. To the spring.

A literal one and hidden deep in an Arkansas thicket where in my early childhood we went, and almost in secret for I never told anybody, to swim.

A Thousand Drippings. That's what the spring was called. The drippings came out of the mountainside. A Thousand Drippings Spring. I still see Rena there so clearly. Rena in the nude, overweight even then by the standards of that day by many pounds. Rena laughing, oblivious to the water moccasins curled against the rocks to the far side.

Uncle Leeland liked the spring as much as Aunt Rena and was as much of a skinny dipper, and he often brought me. When I came along I would step out of my shorts soon enough, (I never in the hot summertime wore a top or shoes) and naked as the day Leona had me, join them. I was scared of the moccasins curled up on the rocks on the spring's far side and yes, they were always there. But Aunt Rena would reassure me.

"They haven't any interest in you," she would say. "They haven't any interest in me. They don't notice much; they are shut up in their skin. But we mustn't scare them. We want them to stay where they are, cool and dreaming. If you keep a good distance and swim quietly by they won't even know you are here."

"Oh, Aunt Rena," I would whisper, "I am such a quiet swimmer."

As I think back on us I realize we were all three of us quiet swimmers. I always went quietly to the spring's deep bottom first thing. The snakes, too, when they slid off the rocks swam quietly, and never for us, though we got out of the water when we saw them getting in. It was a way for all of us to be together, of and with each other in a place near where each of us was born. In no real danger though within sight of it. And sensual without sin.

"I always did think it was all right, his being Jewish," Aunt Rena said to me. "You probably were the right girl for him and I expect he might have made you happy. He was, even back then, different. And you were, too."

"He was only half Jewish," I told her, "and no one in his family practiced the Jewish religion or any other kind."

She told me that we should have probably just run away.

I said, and at that moment at least I thought I was speaking truthfully, that we probably should have. "I was crazy about him," I said, "but we were just children."

"You were seventeen," she said. "I had been married a year when I was seventeen and I had a baby." Then she thought about what she had said; she didn't want me to feel I had taken all the wrong turns or to get discouraged. "Oh, but you have lived in such places," she told me. "All over the country and in Europe and New York. You must have known interesting men, and—"she added after a pause, "cared for some of them."

"I never lived in Europe," I told her. I haven't even done much traveling there." I had, in fact, toured once or twice. "But you are right about this country. I have certainly gotten around."

"And now," Aunt Rena said, "you are way out in Los Angeles. What's it like?"

"Like everything," I told her. "Los Angeles is a country. It has hills and flatlands and desert and ocean." I said although I first lived in the hills I had recently moved to the flats. "It has sunshine and, in the mountains, snow. And many different temperatures. And every kind of tree and person and flower. Oh, Aunt Rena, the oleanders are so thick in August! It would be beautiful," I went on, "If so many hadn't defaced it. And, "I laughed, "If it weren't for all the cars."

I didn't know why I was going into this or what anything I said about Los Angeles could possibly mean to Aunt Rena. But to myself I thought: There are so many possibilities for life in the West, if the big quake doesn't get us or we're not nuked.

"Well," she said, "you must have a lot of fun there."

"It's a work town for me," I told her. "Work is what I know there, what there is to do."

"But you must have a good time, go to the beach, go to shows, go visiting."

I remembered that in four years I hadn't gone to the beach four times or to the theatre or even the movies, at least not just for fun, many more. "Not much," I told her, "not as much as I would do here. What I do there isn't personal."

She just blinked at me. I knew she couldn't comprehend that. "You know," I went on, "all the time I was growing up I was just crazy about radio. I don't know why. Don't ask me why, but all I could think of was that I wanted to work in sound. Well, that's what I do there."

She smiled her sweet, cracked one-hundred-year-old smile which was not very different from her fifty-year-old smile and would be, I decided, not very different from the smile of her invisible ghost. "You like it, though, don't you?"

"It's lonesome, Aunt Rena," I said, "and hard, but yes, I like it."

Then Aunt Rena wanted to know about love, if I had ever been in it. I told her I had been finally. I had not wanted to talk about this at all. But once I got started I knew I had to, for at least a little while, go on. "He was older than I was," I told her, "and, of course, married. Even—" And this was painful for me, "even well married." I stopped. "Whatever that means. Whatever, he was, more or less, I guess. And then," I said, "he got sick and we all lost him, he was an international broadcaster so he belonged to many." Then I stopped. Joe Copeland, I almost said, I'm sure you remember his shows. But I didn't. Aunt Rena wouldn't have listened to Joe's shows much. She didn't say anything. "You see, it wasn't intended." I couldn't go on after that.

"But he cared for you?"

"Yes," I said. "Very much. Very deeply."

I wanted to add, on the deepest level of existence, because I knew that was central and that it was true.

But I couldn't and so, instead, I turned the subject. "Aunt Rena, we might as well face it. An old bachelor brought up an old maid. Not that I blame Uncle Bo. It's hardly his fault."

"Why, honey, you mustn't think that way, people don't think that way anymore." Aunt Rena had always prided herself on keeping up and even at nearly a hundred she knew that anymore no one said "old maid."

"Well," I said, "I just mean that I don't think I was meant to be married or to even live with anyone. Except for you and Uncle Leeland, no one in our family was."

It was her turn to change the subject. "Stay overnight with your Aunt Rena," she said. "Like when you were a little girl and slept with me in the bed. Do you remember how you did that?"

"Oh yes, of course I remember," I told her, "how could I forget?" I always slept with Aunt Rena when Uncle Leeland was away and sometimes when he was home. "It was a feather bed," I told her; "it felt so good and I loved to lie in it and be half asleep in it, just half, I fought sleep because I didn't want to lose awareness of the pleasure."

She laughed. "It did feel good. I haven't had a bed that felt so good since that one."

"I can't stay, Aunt Rena," I told her. "I have to get back to Houston. I have a show to do."

Well, she said she was sorry, then went on to tell me a little of hers and Leeland's story and something more about Lloyd whom I never knew, and more about my mother, Leona. This was the last time I saw Aunt Rena. But I don't know that it's important to give any of that to you.

Right now I have to tell you about Bartola. I just found out while going through an old newspaper file in the UCLA library where I have been researching for a show.

Bartola did finally come to California, lived for awhile in Hollywood, just off Franklin, not far from my first apartment, where not so long ago he was shot through the heart. The shooting disrupted a movie premier; he fell on the walk of fame in front of Mann's Chinese Theatre. The news story I read in the Times talked about the victim being identified as "Bartola Perra" about fifty years old, born in Texas, formerly of San Diego. Although no drugs were found on the body, police believed the victim to be a dealer. He had a history of arrests for performing sexual acts in public. Those interviewed who knew him thought he had lived in California for about five years. I hadn't seen him in more than thirty.

Odd how I thought there could be no truth to a similar report when it was just a rumor back home. Now the only part of the story that strikes me as strange is the brevity of Bartola's life in California. I wondered if he had simply moved from naval base to naval base or spent all his time in you, C.C.

I guessed Bartola had hustled for awhile on the bases, then finally drifted on up to L.A. and made a meager living off Santa Monica Blvd., but I hoped found truer lovers, in Venice, maybe, or even Griffith Park.

Sometimes I think of Hollywood as a place for innocents, for adult children. Full of fantasies. So that when it isn't sheer terror, it's all high school fun.

Near Nacogdoches

I'm back here to visit my mother and my Uncle Bo. Bo is tied to a wheel chair now, having survived, though just barely, a massive coronary and a series of strokes. His doctor says he may live for years.

"He can take a lot," my mother told me. "He's sturdy." But he slumps in his chair and he can't talk much, his bow string seems broken; now sometimes I have to be his speaker. Though on the days when he starts, he still goes on.

"Everything I say may not be true," he tells me. "I hallucinate."

Uncle Bo, I want to tell him, you always did. "You always did," my mother says. Then to me, laughing, as if he isn't there, "He was always telling something."

"Bo," she tells him, "you talk in riddles."

"Well," he says, "you like it."

"His bow is broken," she tells me later. "No song." She considers. "So I guess," she says, "it's up to me to tell you. I am, of the family here, the last." In her eighties, she not only takes care of Bo, but teaches piano to half of the county, has had more students win college scholarships than any of its other teachers, might have helped me win one if I hadn't given up practicing for listening to the radio in eighth grade. "It was Grandaddy's dream, your Grandaddy's, that we come to Texas. 'If you all go to Texas and stay there,' he told me, 'you'll be all right.' And he, he and Leeland, blazed a trail for us. He knew how to do that, had a lot of adventure in him, came to Arkansas from Southern Illinois and to Illinois from Indiana in the 1880s when he was still nearly a boy. His stepmother had taken him out of school and put him in the fields so he had to teach himself and had to travel, had to come south and west for all the country to the south and west needed building. He was born to build, your Grandaddy, and a natural woodsman, and also a natural student and teacher; he was his own teacher, taught himself mathematics and how to read and read a lot, read Poe and Twain and the Bible and he loved newspapers. He loved Arkansas, too, the look of it, though it gave him economic trouble. But, because of all of us, for all of us, Texas gave him ease. 'Honey,' he said, 'you'll be all right, you and Elizabeth and all of you, if you stay in Texas. And I know you're tough enough to stand it.' What he was talking about didn't have a damn thing to do with the oil here, and not much even with making money; he was talking about the effect the country had on people. He knew it was hard on them, would be hard on us: the storms that came out of nowhere, hurricanes some of them, those and the crudity of some of the towns—why the streets in Ingleside weren't even paved when I went there—and the heat, he knew that for six months of the year his children and grandchildren (though you, Elizabeth, turned out to be the only one of these) would have to face that and, God knows, the crudity of some of the people. But he also knew that we all could take it and that taking it would help us continue."

Los Angeles

This brings me to Aunt Rena and maybe to the place where I shouldn't write to you anymore, though it has helped a lot over these last years to be able to.

I began, if you remember, in a cold New York town. There I stayed in a room with a world globe that had a light in it, all the brightness near the center; much of it seemed to come from you, Corpus. So that you appeared to me, not only as the place of my beginning, but as the world's heart.

Then I wrote that first letter and have just rattled on. And it's been good to do that, to know that people like me, wanderers, exiles, drifters, don't have to be homesick always. There is a way to go home.

If "home" means an emotionally charged relationship to only one person, living or dead, and that person is connected to a place, then I think this is still a relevant question. Radio is a way to go back. All the voices come back, all those ever close.

"When I put on those radio plays," I told C.C. "especially when I read a part, I think: Hey, this is for C.C.; she'll be listening." Of course I seldom do them on stations she can pick up.

Did I tell you that on my last trip to Texas I visited C.C. in Kerrville and liked her? And liked her husband who gave me a tour of his kennel. And the room, filled with television monitors and computers, from which he runs it, a charming incongruity: C.C.'s Degas dancers in gilt frames on the walls. And visited with and liked their daughters, a lawyer, an accountant, an elementary school teacher, a young businesswoman and mother of several young children, all of whom live no further away than Austin. And admired a grandchild or two. And several canine friends, Ingrid Bergman, Gary Cooper, named after those radiant presences from our childhood. And the sense of humor that seems to be in the family as well as the kindness and grace.

People can come back together. Those who say something different may not know it.

We all have to ask.

Have to begin by writing a letter. By talking about anything, about the color of the grass where you are from, or the lack of color. Or by asking after the color of the grass you are writing to and miss.

About Aunt Rena: One of her nephews wrote me. In her last year she moved out of her house and in with him and his family. You remember how she spoke of both her nephews as her "little boys."

I am so sorry to inform you about our Aunty. She passed away on Jan 1, at 12:30 p.m. and is at peace and out of pain. Her heart just quit. All at once stopped.

We put her away very nice as she asked us to. And me and my brother and our wives have spaces next to hers. And all our children in an adjoining plot.

So sorry to bear this news. We all loved her so much.

It was signed, "I remain in sorrow, Searcy." That is his name, Searcy. I laughed aloud at the sound of it and when I read that Aunt Rena had asked to be put away "nice." Then I wrote to say I hoped to soon visit Louisiana. I said I hoped I could come to Aunt Rena's grave with a picnic lunch on a pretty spring day, that I wanted to get to know him and his wife and his brother and wife and all their children, or at least to get to know them a little, although I didn't say this, for as little as a weekend or a day. And that I was sorry that over all the years I never had. "Why, you must remember Searcy," I now recall Aunt Rena saying once, and I didn't, "When you were little he carried you out back to the creek and once all the way to the spring."

Maybe when I make this trip I'll also drop down to see you, Corpus, and never mind what that woman said to me about you on the train. I hear you're still very pretty, some say prettier than ever and more fun, a jazz festival in the summer, a Bayfest in the fall, new hotels on your shoreline.

I hope to stay in one soon. Next year, maybe. In March, maybe; I'm scheduled to travel then. Yes, it will be March when I leave for Texas. The very next time I go.

About the Author

Eve La Salle Caram has published a set of "Corpus Christi" Novels, *Dear Corpus Christi* and *Rena, a Late Journey* and is working on a third. She is also the author of the short novel, *Wintershine* and the editor of *Palm Readings, Stories from Southern California*. She teaches Literature and Writing at California State University at Northbridge, fiction writing in the Writers' Program at UCLA and has taught writing at a number of colleges and unversities. A new novel, *The Blue Geography*, is forthcoming. She grew up in South Texas.